Whispers
on the Hampstead Road

The Scoundrel of Mayfair book 4

Vivian Roycroft

δ
Dingbat Publishing
Humble, Texas

WHISPERS ON THE HAMPSTEAD ROAD
Copyright © 2015 by Vivian Roycroft
Primary print ISBN 9-798-8-39291263

Published by Dingbat Publishing
Humble, Texas

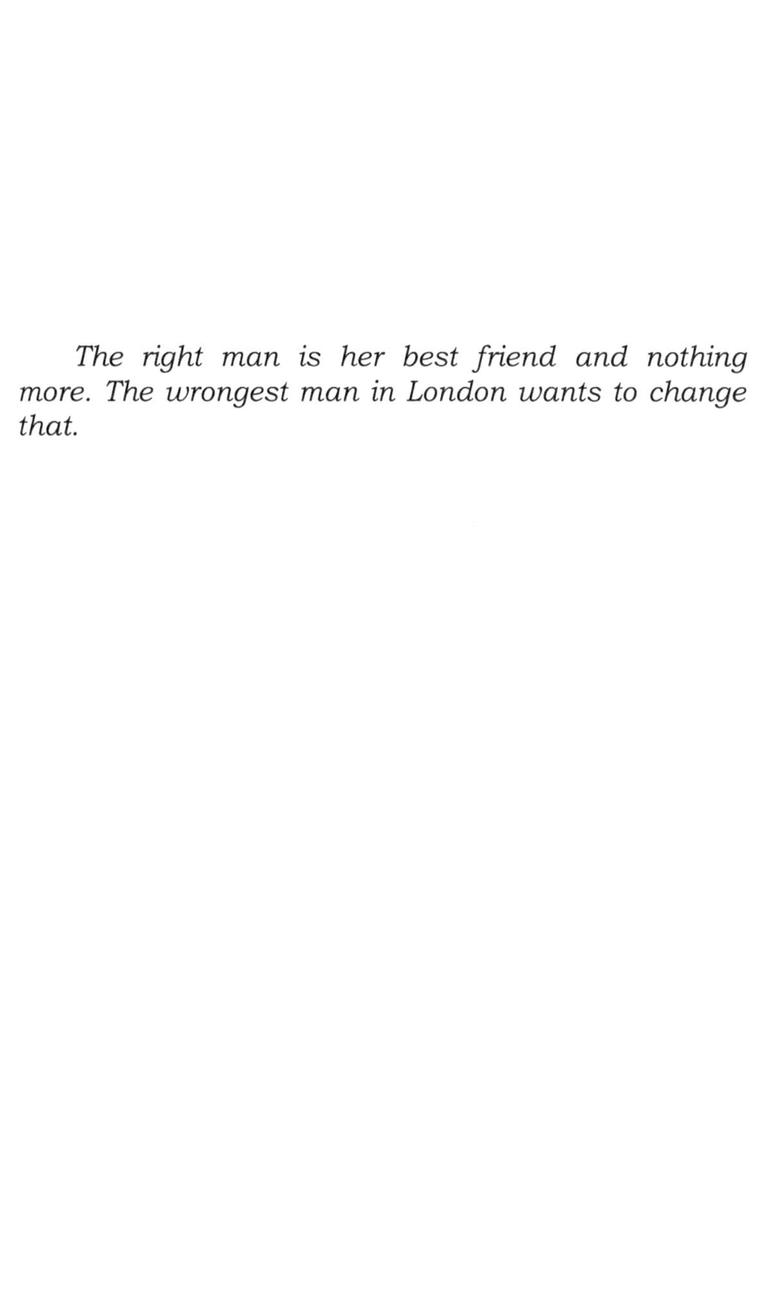

The right man is her best friend and nothing more. The wrongest man in London wants to change that.

Prologue

Deborah

May 7, 1813

It was one of the year's first fine spring days, a day when the pale sun's warmth wasn't overwhelmed by a blustery wind. It was the sort of day when the female animals peered sideways back at the always-staring males. And Deborah Kringle found herself staring, too.

She stood on the sidelines at Rotten Row, minding her own business (no matter what anyone else might say), and the most gorgeous man ever born trotted past on a splendid grey hunter.

Athletic, he was, trim of waist and broad of shoulder, and his beautifully curved calves wrapped around the hunter's barrel as if they'd been designed for that purpose. Distracting little curly wisps of dark hair tempted at his nape. Even the whorl of his ear made her fingers itch to explore him. No man who looked that good had any business being allowed out in public without a bodyguard, especially not on such a wonderful, fresh spring day.

Then she blinked and awakened, as if from the loveliest dream, and found herself staring calf-eyed at George Anson.

George Anson.

Oh. *Oh.* Deborah felt the disaster in her bones. She couldn't be more mortified if she'd awakened to find herself dancing naked atop the dining room table in front of her parents and nineteen guests. After all, there were some situations where a girl's reputation simply couldn't recover. Staring at George Anson had to top that list.

She managed to straighten her face before the next set of hoofbeats arrived. With her chin held level in demure innocence, she met the new rider's eye—and shriveled inside.

She'd been *seen.* And there was no getting out of it this time.

The Duke of Cumberland—clever, knowing, dangerous man—stared back at her, his eyes wide, as if he couldn't believe her behavior, either. Beneath his disbelief danced a bit of mischief, and his gaze lingered on her face far longer than society considered proper.

Then, before she could swoon for sympathy, he drew in a deep breath, shrugged, shook the reins, and his big dark stallion snorted and thundered away down the track in George Anson's wake.

Deborah

She crawled into bed that night still a nervous wreck, heart thudding, certain to the core of her being that she would never, ever live down that moment, that *insane* moment when *George Anson* had seemed like the man to have. Surely her name would be in every gossip sheet in Mayfair over the next week. Surely her pitiful situation would be discussed in every coffee house, pub, dinner party, and entertainment in the city.

It took a week before Deborah realized that her nightmare was not coming true. Her name graced no gossip sheet, and if anyone discussed her moment of insanity, the whispers never reached her ears. She began to relax, and her mother soon had no reason to ask if she were feeling poorly, with the return of her appetite and insatiable desire for coffee and oolong.

Another week passed before she figured out why. A rake His Grace might be, but a gossip, never. Although it was quite possible that he'd decided nobody would believe such a story—Deborah Kringle sighing after George Anson, forsooth—which would defeat any potential purpose in telling the tale. In any case, as spring gave way to summer and autumn, she heard nary a whisper nor felt a stare.

But still, she hadn't been able to meet His Grace's whimsical gaze until August.

Chapter One

His Grace

Wednesday afternoon, November 17, 1813

A dry, crisp bite chilled the air. His Grace paused outside Trent's coffee house and eyed the door, pursing his lips. Stopping in for a warming cup held a certain attraction, although the accompanying social necessities would impinge upon his afternoon plans.

Ahead, smoky Coralie didn't notice him or his indecision, but then, she hadn't yet noticed his presence and he'd trailed them all the way from the Strand. She continued on her determined way, her fur-trimmed pelisse flaring around her alluring form as she strode into the lively breeze that whispered along Fleet Street. The sweet yellow roses bedecking her bonnet bobbed with the wind and a delicate blond curl danced on her elegant collar. She pointed across the street, and Rainier, escorting her with one hand clapped to his beaver, peered through the sparse shoppers toward her chosen target. He nodded, hand and hat moving ludicrously together, then they threaded past a pack of giggling debutantes, waited for a break in the phaetons and curricles, and trotted across the street together.

Ernst Anton Oldenburg, His Grace, the Duke of Cumberland (and some said a foreign prince) let them go. The former Miss Coralie Busche, now Mrs. Rainier, never glanced away from her objective, the Robinsons' linen-draper shop, in her serene confidence leaving her husband to fend off such trivialities as clattering, onrushing carriages—and from the sound of it, a big one rapidly approached. Rumor around Mayfair, as reported by the *Chatterer*, said the new Mrs. Rainier, comfortably settled and in full charge of the home, intended to modernize the upstairs. Mayfair's most popular fabric store seemed an appropriate starting point.

But as her rippling hemline vanished into the shop's interior, her husband paused on the threshold and glanced back, as if somewhere along their path he'd felt His Grace's sustained stare and thought it time to return the favor. The big carriage passed between them, three pairs of greys, trotting hoofs, gilt and shining varnish flashing in the autumn sunlight. Then its motion whirled away and the pavement stretched, suddenly empty, across to where Rainier hesitated by the diamond-paned windows. His Grace waited. Rainier nodded an awkward greeting and tipped his beaver, setting his brown curls at the breeze's mercy. A sartorial mistake, considering how long Rainier's valet had to have spent arranging those curls, and His Grace couldn't say he was tempted to reciprocate. A nod returned the greeting, a touch to his own hat brim, then the moment passed and Rainier followed his wife into the shop, the footman closing the door behind them.

Breathtaking Coralie's adventure had ended. Her dream had come true in all its complex layers.

And that left him free to acquire his next target.

As his lips curled in satisfaction, a deep voice shouted a playful challenge from somewhere down

Fleet Street, the wind whipping the call along toward the Strand. A feminine squeal answered. Along the pavement in front of the shops and stores, everyone's heads turned as hurrying shoppers paused in their chilly rush and peered past the sign for Clark and Weatherly, goldsmiths. On the sidewalk across the street from Trent's, a pair of dandies laughed at something still out of sight for His Grace.

His smile deepened. No, he couldn't see them, not yet. But in the prim and proper West Side, surely only one couple would dare play public pranks that led to squeals, shouts, and laughter? His accidental timing seemed perfect.

And the coffee could wait.

A flash of emerald green rounded the goldsmiths' corner at a gallop and jolted to a sudden stop. A pelisse, it was, and of course no one else could possibly have been wearing it. Deborah Kringle's eyes widened in surprise, as if she couldn't believe anyone would pause and stare at innocent little her. She whipped her hands and whatever they held behind her back—and then startled and whirled as a grinning George Anson appeared beside her, yanking his hat from her grip and settling it upon his head where it belonged. He grimaced at her in playful reproach, tapped the hat's top in victory, then grabbed it and held on as the breeze joined their game. Deborah laughed at him. After a moment to secure his prize, Anson joined in.

Although their families had of course known each other forever, it had only been mid October, a bare month ago, the first time Deborah yanked Anson's hat from his head and ran down the street, shrieking and ducking between carriages and pedestrians, inviting him to chase her and defiantly daring anyone to scold her outrageous behavior. Any number of adorable biddies had, of course, reproving or at least attempting to reprove Deborah and her regal, tolerant mother, Lady Kringle, both separately and together. But as anyone with less solemnity could have warned the dear chaperones in advance, their harsh words fell upon two sets of uncaring ears.

Since that day, Deborah's favorite prank had become a common occurrence, often interrupting Mayfair's sometimes boring propriety. Even before then, her interactions with Anson had long grown steadily more playful, more intimate. And last spring he'd noticed...

But he had no time for daydreaming. The two friends approached him, sauntering side by side along the pavement, emerging from beneath the shadow of St.-Dunstan's-in-the-West and talking earnestly as they came. For a moment they were bathed in cold sunshine, her hair lightening to spun gold and the pastel ribbons on her daringly open bonnet glowing. Strong contrast, that, against Anson's sober and respectable brown coat and trousers, and perhaps symbolic of their relationship— she daringly led and he willingly followed.

Then the bookseller's awning dropped them back into shade. They both glanced ahead, away from their sustained conversation, and paused when they noticed him watching and waiting outside Trent's. Their coordination couldn't have been more perfect if they'd practiced those movements for years.

As if they were already long married. And yet...

Some expression must have crossed his face, for Deborah's cheerful recognition morphed into a rueful, sheepish grimace, part guilt and part mischief— for all the world like a child who'd been caught at a dastardly prank. His Grace couldn't stop his smile from responding. He'd seen what he'd seen last spring, and she'd never convince him otherwise, no matter how many grimaces she sent his way.

"Your grace." Anson touched his hat brim, keeping his hair under control; no fool he, although some overly educated sorts chose to see him as one. "A pleasure."

Twelve months ago, His Grace might have responded to a greeting from Anson with a measure of amiable contempt. But the prancing buffoon who'd been widely mocked at last year's Holly Hall Christmas Eve ball, the one who'd been trying so hard to impress Deborah that he'd made a joke of himself, had matured much in the intervening time. No one would go so far as to describe him as sober and responsible—much less intellectual, and His Grace smiled again at the thought. But Anson had grown into his skin. He accepted himself as he was and no longer sought to become someone, anyone else.

His Grace nodded in return. "A pleasure indeed, Mr. Anson."

The wary surprise that swept Anson's face—and the wary horror on Deborah's—was its own reward.

George Anson and Deborah Kringle—a perplexing situation, between the two of them. They were obviously the best of friends, well matched, comfortable in their relationship, and fully content. And yet they refused to take the next step beyond friendship. Anson refused to express his not entirely secret desire for her. She refused to make more plain the esteem in which she held him. It was as if they were content to be nothing more than friends and pranksters for the rest of their lives—as if they were content to never experience more than the merest shadow of love.

But how to begin a game with their marriage as the prize? A boorish challenge from him would yield nothing beyond the push back from Deborah it would so richly deserve. And his usual gambit, pretending to woo the young lady and forcing the gentleman's hand via the subtle knife of jealousy, would patently fall flat before their joint determination. No, he needed some new trick, some discreet indiscretion, to coerce this stubborn pair into motion. But what?

A deep breath, and His Grace eased his knowing smile—very well, his *smirk* into more charming lines. He bowed to Deborah. "My dear Miss Kringle, how are the preparations for this year's Christmas Eve ball progressing? Everyone who's anyone awaits an invitation with bated breath."

She bobbed a curtsey. "Including you?" When he shot his eyebrows, she rushed on, a conversational parry and retreat. "Honestly, I've no idea. Mama rattles on about it every night, but my poor brain shuts down within a minute. How she keeps track of it all, I cannot say."

"Well, it's a prodigious undertaking." Anson puffed out his chest; he'd slipped a big word or two into the conversation, and he'd gotten them right, too. He eyed her sideways. "You should be helping her, you know."

With a huff, Deborah blew out her cheeks. "As if Mama wants any assistance from me. She'd much rather I come to town and run errands for her." She rolled her eyes at His Grace, half a shrug at Anson's silliness and half a plea for patience on his behalf. "And as that's what I'm supposed to be doing now, I must bid you adieu, your grace." Another bobbed curtsey, then she grabbed Anson's arm and, with barely a pause for him to stammer his own farewell, she hauled him away.

Summarily dismissed—oh, and his smirk had deserved it, too—His Grace laughed and let them go, turning and watching them depart. Anson glanced back over his shoulder, a puzzled line creasing his broad forehead in purely masculine confusion. He'd understood none of the young lady's conversational nuances. Then her grip on his arm tightened, tugging him beside her down the sidewalk toward the City.

The moment passed, and with it His Grace's concentration. Fleet Street broadened around him, the voices and rattling and bustling returning to his awareness. The unusually insistent sunlight bathed the chariotway to his right; the bookseller's canopy blocked it from the sidewalk. Behind him, the clock bells of St. Dunstan's-in-the-West began tolling the hour, long sonorous notes falling heavily on the street. Fainter echoes from more distant churches chimed in with a soft melody. Suddenly it all seemed so strange, so different from home—as if he hadn't resided in London for the past seven years, as if he'd stepped off the boat from the north German shores only that minute.

A massive trotting and rattling approached from behind and he glanced over his shoulder. The big carriage and three pairs of greys returned, coming back the way they'd gone. A clever eye indeed had paired off the mares, for all six trotted in near unison, forelegs reaching and stepping together, and all of them boasted similar size and breeding. The enclosed carriage, dark varnish and shine, velvet drapes pulled across, loomed above the staring pedestrians—including him, and he had more important things to do than stand and ogle some rich person's equipage.

But a golden glint on the door made His Grace pause again. A heraldic shield marked the carriage, white with plain ermine in gold instead of black—the duchy of Bretagne, or Brittany, as the English called it. Openly he stared as the greys and their big burden advanced along Fleet Street. Six years ago, while he'd been training with the King's German Legion, the Duchess of Brittany had escaped with the noble Duke of Orléans and a general whose political allegiance had balked at the change from revolution to Napoleon. She'd taken Chelmsford House, Piccadilly, he'd heard, and clearly now she employed an excellent master of horse.

He'd made it a point to avoid the French *émigrés* in London, mainly because it was said their meetings had become a hotbed of whispered political secrets, a hotbed best avoided. But clearly the Duchess of Brittany was becoming a presence in Mayfair. Perhaps he'd call on her, if she offered a weekly drawing room. He shrugged and the greys and carriage swept past, a sudden thunder of enclosed noise, just as quickly gone beyond the goldsmith's. Well, perhaps, and then again, perhaps not.

Something, some flash of motion, drew his eye to the street's far side. For a moment it all swam together in the brighter light, the hurrying pedestrians, the dazzle off the linen-draper's diamond panes, the dizzying whirl of a phaeton's wheels in passing. Then the world righted itself and a small, slight figure in a flaring cloak passed beyond the goldsmiths' corner, following the carriage's path. A swift impression of a deeply cowled hood, a gracefully whirling hemline, and then she was gone, whoever she was.

Several times since those fey October nights had he seen the same lithe form, but only at a distance, only from the side or back. Never had he been blessed with a clear view; never had she deigned to approach him more closely; and never had she appeared without that all-encompassing cloak. She moved like his beloved Ursula, so much so that he yearned to chase after her. But he would not, for it could not be her.

That meant he'd been fooled, back in October, by the uncertain light and the ghostly atmosphere. The thought rankled. He'd have sworn the feat was impossible, that he'd have picked his beloved's form, her grace, her stunning beauty, from any crowd, at any distance. But if she'd seen him across the street, be it ten times as busy and dangerous as Fleet Street, she'd have run to him as he'd run to her. Ursula would *not* have slipped away and left him forlorn.

He shook himself and pursed his lips, returning his thoughts to Deborah and Anson. His first instinct seemed accurate. The usual threatened dalliance would not serve. Deborah would enjoy the flirtation he offered and put him in his place when she tired of the game. Anson would wear the normal lines of male befuddlement and carry on. And once His Grace's play was over, the two of them would return to their merry ways, no further advanced than before.

He needed something special here, something unusual and striking, something they couldn't ignore. The game wasn't on yet, but he'd find a way to make it so.

Chapter Two

Wednesday evening, November 17, 1813
The Honorable Deborah Kringle brooded.

It was her parents' fault. Well, maybe not her parents, but definitely her grandparents, the paternal pair who took the silly name Kringle, gave unrestrained vent to their fascination with Christmas—and built their stately town house on the open road to the countryside instead of in town. Their lack of foresight had landed her well outside Mayfair, well away from all her friends, and nowhere close to any of the evening entertainments. And it wasn't as if they'd built on a particularly large tract of land. They could just as easily have erected the same house with the same formal garden on, say, Duke Street, or Warwick. Instead, they'd opted for the Hampstead Road, beside the old chapel and its burying ground.

The graveyard. She discreetly shuddered.

Not discreetly enough. Lady Kringle eyed her over the polished silver tray and handed her the first cup of coffee, steady in its moving saucer. "If you're cold, dear, pull your chair closer to the fire."

Deborah accepted the cup. The first creamy sip

warmed her mouth and soothed her nerves. "I was thinking about our neighbors."

Mama paused, the silver pot poised over her cup. "The Stanfords? What on earth could be objectionable about that lovely young couple?"

"Not them, the burying ground."

"If you remind me one more time that we live in the *dead center of nowhere*, you'll get no more coffee tonight." Mama poured, settled the pot on the tray, and applied herself to lumps and cream.

She never appreciates my punderful lines. Deborah sighed. Hopefully she hid that better than the shudder.

If her benighted grandparents had only thought ahead and considered her future needs, then she would not be pouting at home, with nothing to do but sit in the withdrawing room after dinner while Papa finished his brandy. Honestly, that was the real problem, not Mama's unending chatter about preparations for the Christmas Eve ball. It was the boredom. She had no agreeable distractions, nor any disagreeable ones, for that matter, leaving her with all too much spare time. And during that empty time, her mind insisted upon remembering what had happened back in May.

Anson. George Anson. And she'd been seen by the worst possible witness.

Another shudder tried to ripple down her spine. She quenched it with more coffee. She would never admit that His Grace had seen anything, and he, and his smirk, could go hang if he thought otherwise.

A clink from the tray, and Mama sat back, cup and saucer in hand. "Besides," she said, "if you object to your current living arrangements, all you need do is marry."

Deborah froze. There were moments when Mama seemed to understand Deborah's thoughts in her bones. But surely—*surely* she had not given herself away. And not even that dangerous duke would have taken such gossip to her *parents...* would he?

Mama's serene attention never wavered, and a cold wash of fear drenched Deborah's innards. Then again, maybe he had. Where else had Mama gotten such a dreadful idea? Marriage? Truly?

But before she could think of a defense, the butler entered, salver held before him. "Forgive the intrusion, madam."

Mama drew back, eyebrows rising. "Mail at this hour, Ames?"

Deborah returned to her cooling coffee. It could only be something to do with the ball, not a distraction for her.

"No, madam." He glided across the Axminster carpet, footfalls soundless and smooth. But when Mama held out her hand, he discreetly altered course.

A message for... for *her*? Deborah's pulse picked up speed. *Oh, how lovely.*

The folded ivory-colored paper was thick and expensive, the ink deep blue with powdered indigo, the seal crimson and scented faintly with balsam of Peru. It must have been hand-delivered, since they hadn't overheard the frantic racket of an arriving express. She didn't recognize the handwriting, although it seemed vaguely familiar, as if she'd seen it long before and simply couldn't bring its identification into clear focus. "An invitation? Who brought it, Ames?"

The butler paused at the door. "He wore no livery, miss."

Mama sipped her coffee with her usual serenity, but her sharp eyes never left the folded paper. "There's one easy way of ascertaining the sender."

Keeping her cheeky response to herself, Deborah broke the seal and unfolded the heavy creases. She took a deep breath in preparation for reading aloud, but the first word died in her throat. Rapidly she skimmed the few brief paragraphs, and all notions of boredom and pouting vanished in a heartbeat.

"Dear? Is anything wrong?"

She glanced up. Curiosity rolled from Mama's beady-eyed stare in waves, but the curl of her lip hinted she'd already guessed at the missive's contents.

"Oh, no, just something silly from—from Lissie McTaggart." Deborah started refolding the letter, but couldn't resist another peak down when Mama turned away to pour a second cup.

Love suffereth long, and is courteous, the Good Book tells us, and long have I suffered beneath my love for you. *Love dealeth not dishonestly,* it says, and yet for longer than I believed possible, my love remained successfully hidden from your beautiful, gracious eyes. Because it's no longer possible to withstand this cruel and sweet infirmity, because *love rejoiceth in the truth,* I must needs...

"Miss Lissie's silliness seems fairly engrossing."

A hasty scrabble, and Deborah tucked the refolded letter into her glove. "Trust me, I'm giving it far more attention than it deserves." She couldn't possibly share such a letter with anyone, certainly not her mother. Not yet, at least; not until she'd savored its ringing syllables in the quiet of her room and hugged them to herself.

A love letter. She'd received a love letter, written in vaguely familiar handwriting, using wildly expensive indigo ink, on the thickest wove paper available.

For a certainty, it wasn't written by anyone cheap. Unfortunately, that was all she knew, because the letter, the exquisite love letter, had been sent unsigned.

She needed to remember the author of that hand. A feverish excitement flushed through her and she nearly shivered again. There had to be a way to discover who wrote it. But how?

Thankfully, she knew just who to ask. And tomorrow morning couldn't come soon enough.

Anson

Thursday morning, November 18, 1813

The sun was barely peeping above the neighboring roofs, and already Anson was moping over the breakfast table. It was a terrible way for a grown man to live, and yet there it was.

Women. He would never understand them, and the thought threatened to curdle the tea in his stomach.

George Anson prided himself on not being conspicuously different from the other gentlemen about town. He'd had the proper upbringing and education, even if he hadn't been the brightest star in that particular sky, and his bespoke tailor had standing orders to keep him sporting the best of taste, sartorially speaking. All right, so French remained a mystery, symphonies left him nodding, and Horace Walpole's latest attracted him far more than any of the rubbish he'd been ordered to memorize at Eton. For all that, he could bowl a straight wicket and his grey hunter could beat all but the Master's chestnut to the kill. And he bagged more birds than anyone else every year. He knew for a fact that even Cumberland, that cunning dog of war, admired his shooting skills.

Just as important, even before inheriting he had five thousand per annum, with the capital so locked up amongst the estate that even if he'd been of a mind to gamble it away, he'd never survive the red tape to reach it. He would die amidst endless coils of lawyers' entanglements first.

So all things considered, he wasn't a bad catch. Perhaps he couldn't debate philosophy with Kenneth Rainier, or literature with Frederick Shaw, or anything with... well, anyone. None of that intellectual stuff could possibly be as important as bringing his chestnut filly home the winner at Goodwood next spring, which he had every intention of doing.

And yet women looked down their noses at him. All of them. Not one or two, but every gentlewoman worth the catching thought him a good-natured buffoon, at best.

He danced with all the right people at all the right balls. He was seen at symphonies for as long as he could prop his eyelids open, and even spent polite time with Lady Gower, that feminine tiger of predatory fame. He never left his behavior open to censure—well, almost never—and never followed Culver's ruinous, rakish lead nor, saints forbid, Cumberland's. He never dressed in last year's trousers. And he never, ever breathed a word of his secret. Only his valet knew of... *that,* and Vicker was far too generously paid to permit treasonous behavior. Besides, Vicker's mother was housekeeper on the old estate; if he betrayed his master, Vicker would hear about it from a much stronger source than George Anson.

And yet...

Sweet Anne Kirkhoven used to stare at him with her eyebrows creeping slowly higher when they'd chatted at the coffee house, as if she hadn't believed the things coming from his mouth. Lissie McTaggart willingly danced with him, but then, she was nice to everyone, even stray dogs and orphans. Beryl Wentworth had smiled at him once, but she'd also once adopted a broken-down cart horse. Besides, with that smile she'd shown every sign of trying to make old Fitzwilliam jealous—not that she'd succeeded, not with *him* as her decoy. He even knew what they called him—the Honorably Abominable George Anson.

And Deborah Kringle…

Anson sighed. Deborah Kringle. A leggy wood nymph with tall elegance, brilliant eyes, the wickedest sense of humor, and twenty thousand pounds in the ten percents. She'd had the nerve to wear a scarlet gown to her parents' Christmas Eve ball last year, and he'd not missed her sneer at his simple, sober, conventional black swallowtail. They'd opened the ball together—what a blessed thrill that had been!—but before the evening's conclusion, she had been on Cumberland's arm, half of the most elegant couple in the room.

And he'd ended the evening standing against the wall with the bluestockings, listening to Deborah and Cumberland's discussion of Plutarch, if he remembered correctly. How he'd yearned to contribute something intelligent to their conversation.

But some things just weren't going to happen, were they?

Deborah had been a delightful friend for the last twelve-month. She'd invited him over for tea, sat and laughed with him after family dinners, and even lately she'd taken to snatching his hat from his head and playing chase with him down Fleet Street to the Strand. Everyone stared, and for a while all the gossips had waited for a next, matrimonial sort of step in their relationship.

But the weeks passed. Nothing further happened. She continued her playful, bantering ways, never once giving him soft looks or wistful eyes, and the gossip had stopped. For he would never risk spoiling their friendship by trying to be romantic. Rejection from anyone else wasn't personal, or so he could tell himself, but rejection from Deborah would be catastrophic.

Well. Perhaps she'd let him open the Christmas Eve ball with her again this year. There was that possibility to look forward to.

Anson folded his napkin and set it beside his plate as the butler entered, silver salver bearing a note. A thrill shot through him. He knew that plain pale blue paper as well as he knew his own salmon laid with the crest.

Seemed there was hope for the day yet.

"Thank'ee, Sandringham." Anson popped the wax seal and unfolded the note:

The most excellent mystery appeared at the Kringle door last evening and the adventure to ensue promises to be just as thrilling. Tea shall be ready for eleven and Cook has baked spice cookies.

Deborah's tiny signature was adorned with so many whorls and flourishes, it covered half the little paper. His lips curled in a grin. That woman stamped her brilliant personality on everything she touched.

If only she'd stamp a bit on him.

"Sandringham, I'll need Plato for half past nine and my blue Melton before then. The Kringle tea table awaits."

Chapter Three

Deborah

Thursday, November 18, 1813

The morning room glowed golden with pure winter sunlight, but already the first grey cloud approached... *from the burying ground.* Deborah hid her shudder with a stretch. Then, before Mama could inquire, she bent again over her needlework. If that cloud invited its friends along for the journey and they darkened the sky, it would be impossible to see well enough to sew, and Papa needed these new collars, no matter where the clouds came from.

Besides, a good sleep and several strong black cups of oolong had clarified her thoughts on solving last evening's mystery. It all came down to the handwriting. Before she could draw any lasting conclusions from that lovely letter, she had to determine who wrote it, and since her memory refused to divulge the penman's identity, she'd have to find other ways of figuring it out.

Sewing or no, waiting for George's arrival was a trial, because he was bound to have some good ideas for sorting things out. Marriage material he might not be, but he made a first-class conspirator.

From the chair nearby, Mama's knitting needles clacked, a steady rhythm like a metallic heartbeat. Speaking of possibilities...

"Mama," she said, "for how many years have you and Papa been hosting the Christmas Eve ball?"

Clack clack clack, and the pale yellow strip of whatever Mama was making seemed to have grown by a foot while Deborah had taken a handful of careful stitches. She *would* be stuck with the slow project. Some days, life simply wasn't fair.

"It's coming up on two decades now, since your father's mother's passing, when I assumed the role." The clacking punctuated her syllables. "Nineteen years, this Christmas." *Clack clack clack.* "Someday I hope *one of my daughters* will take over the running of such a proud tradition."

Just the barest, most genteel of emphases on that phrase, nearly inaudible amongst the *clack clack clacking.*

Deborah refrained from sniffing. That subject was not what she wanted to discuss. And if Mama thought her capable of running *that* ball, well, perhaps she didn't know her own daughter as well as she imagined. "I was wondering..." Needle properly aligned along the established seam, she slid it triumphantly through and settled another stitch—one single stitch—into place.

"Ye-es?" *Clack clack clack.*

"You wouldn't happen to have kept the answered invitations through all those years, would you?" It came out in a rush of words, not the calm sentence she'd hoped for. Deborah cringed. Mama could scent a scheme a mile away. If she became suspicious...

No, the letter would remain her secret. Well, hers and George's, soon enough. But he hardly counted.

It took Deborah a moment to realize that the sound she heard was silence. She glanced up.

Mama stared at her, eyebrows soaring up her forehead. The knitting needles were still for the first time that hour. "Why on earth would I have kept them?"

Oh, dear. Deborah thought fast. "I just thought of all the history involved. The *feminine* history. Not battles or wars, but dance floors, you know."

Another long stare. Finally Mama's gaze lowered back to her work and the clacking resumed. The pale yellow project she labored over seemed to be taking a turn, like a curving road. A bed sock; it had to be a bed sock. Well, winter was coming, after all.

"No," Mama finally said. "I cannot say I foresaw the need. Each year, the answered invitations assist in starting the new year's first fire."

And that sounded like yet another tradition surrounding the fabled Christmas Eve ball. Deborah sighed. No, she would never be able to assume hosting the ball in Mama's stead. She would never remember all the silly traditions involved. Ivy and holly collected from *the burying ground* the afternoon prior, new gowns and livery for all the staff, new vanilla-scented candles precisely every two feet along the banquet table's center, a decorated tree with presents in the family parlor to please Cumberland... there wasn't a book large enough to hold all the details. And Mama had never written them all down. How on earth the woman did it—

No, saved invitations had been too much to expect, and a lucky stroke she would not have deserved. She'd have to await George's arrival. He would have the perfect idea; she just knew it.

Anson

Plato, his good grey hunter, followed the groom around Holly Hall toward the stable in back, tugging against the reins with an eye on the still-green lawn. Anson grinned. Hopefully the man would turn the poor beast out for a graze. A hunter was wasted in the city, of course, but at least the constant exercise of riding about town kept Plato fit. And they'd be headed home after the Holly Hall Christmas Eve ball, in any case, so the horse would be ready for some rousing gallops then.

Before him rose Holly Hall in all its elegance, windows sparkling and pinkish stone gleaming from wing to battlemented wing. Steps curved in two rounded arcs from the paved drive to the unsheltered front entrance and its carved oak double doors. On either side of the entry were niches holding Grecian-type statues, one male, one female. The statues were supposed to be Apollo and Diana, but rumor had it the original Lord and Lady Kringle, Deborah's grandparents, had immortalized themselves so. Some people believed it; some didn't. Certainly more than a trifle of resemblance existed between the two statues and the portraits in the gallery, though.

But the house boasted so little land. A formal garden, a kitchen garden, the knot garden for herbs, a little wilderness surrounded by brick walls, a pasture for horses and a goodly chunk of that taken over by the palatial stable block. Not a parcel when compared to his family's country place in Oxfordshire, with its acres stretching near to the horizon and old-growth woods to shelter the wildlife.

No, Holly Hall was lovely and all that, but there wasn't enough land and so it could never be a fit home for Deborah. With her boundless energy and enthusiasm, she needed more room to romp and play out of doors—some place to ride, a lake to skate on, fish in, even swim in when no one was looking. Surely someday she'd see that, see that he had something to offer her that she didn't already have.

Someday. Perhaps.

Hope rose in him yet again, a pleased pressure in his chest. He seemed to live for *someday.*

Anson climbed the steps and rang the bell. Ames led him past the gallery's arched entry, through the main foyer, big enough in itself to hold a ball of some size, up the sweeping staircase to the mansion's rear, where the morning room stretched to the open windows and sunlight gilded the air.

Exquisite in a frowzy, rumpled old blue gown, Deborah sat behind a work table at one window, framed by the ivory draperies and bathed in gold. A soft breeze played with her pale curls. He wanted to stop and admire her—well, didn't he always?—but she spotted him before he could even pause.

"Oh, good, you're here." A bounce to her feet for a bow-curtsey exchange, then she waved him to the chair opposite hers. Barely was he seated, unable to stifle his idiotic grin, than she pushed a sheet of paper toward him. Automatically his glance dropped and followed the motion.

Anson froze.

It... could only be a joke. Another of Deborah's pranks, something she'd cooked up for a laugh. But when he glanced back up at her, he saw what his delight had before hidden from him—a strange sort of excitement that radiated from her like heat from pavement, a glitter in her delightful eyes that he had never seen in her before.

Tension, cautious as a hunting cat, began twisting around his heart.

"Go on." She leaned forward, and he couldn't stop his automatic glance down toward her bosom. "Go *on*, George. Read it."

He didn't want to. But he did, and his coiling tension morphed into anger, stronger with each succeeding, ridiculous word. An anonymous love letter, some imbecile pouring out his heart with devotion and idiotic romantic sentiments, gushing silliness across the poor undeserving paper as if the writer had nothing—*nothing!*—to hide.

Clearly it was a fake. That first morbid glance had told him that. It could only be a fake, somebody laughing Deborah up, and Anson's anger expanded, filling him like one of those hot air balloons popping up all over the place.

Because what looked back at him from the note was his own handwriting.

And he hadn't written it.

Deborah

Deborah frowned. Odd, the way George had clammed up, lips pressed into a thin line, while he'd read her love letter. Surely he hadn't noticed her weak-kneed, calf-eyed moment back in May. No, surely not. Well, it didn't matter if he had, for she had no intention of ever admitting to it. Some things a girl's reputation just couldn't survive.

Instead she leaned forward and reached across the table, rubbing the expensive paper. It barely gave beneath her fingers' pressure, testament to its thickness and quality. "Who on earth might have written this?"

He cleared his throat and pushed the paper back toward her, rather as he might shove away an asp. "No idea."

"We need to determine whose handwriting this is. Toward that end, I asked Mama if she'd kept the answered invitations from all the Christmas Eve balls of the past nineteen years." A twist of her wrist turned the love letter around to face her. The deep blue ink showed so beautifully against the gentle ivory; perhaps she should change her stationery, or at least her ink. "But of course she didn't, and then I had to concoct a reason for such an outlandish request." Still George didn't smile. If he relished her mystery and the coming adventure, he hid it well. "Aren't you curious? At all?"

Finally he lifted his face and shifted in his chair. Anger smoldered in his eyes, adding a whiff of fire to their usual good-natured brown. "No, not a whit." His voice grated, rough and angry. "Likely some fool with too much time on his hands and not enough responsibility."

What on earth? George Anson, angry? She'd never seen it before. Strange, how part of her wanted to soothe his temper away... and how another, bigger part wanted to tease it to a hotter blaze, just to learn what George in a tempest was like. "Well, that's lovely, that is. I'd intended asking you to help me figure this out, you know."

"Oh, I'll help you figure this out, all right. And then I'll plant a fist in the blithering fool's face."

No, that temper didn't need teasing. "What makes you think the situation calls for violence?"

He stared back, eyes flashing, brows soaring. "You'd permit this sort of flirtation?"

How to fluster a girl, in one easy lesson. Deborah looked back down at the love letter, uncertain what to say. "Well, it's hardly flirtation if it's only on paper, is it?"

A grunt. Or perhaps more of a scoff. "You never did care for your reputation. You should, you know. It's the only one you'll ever have, and once it's ruined, it's gone."

She couldn't help but laugh. Good old George. "Surely that poor thing died the moment I first snatched your hat and ran down Piccadilly with it, you hot on my heels. Face it, George, I've been ruined in that manner for years, and you helped accomplish that singular feat." Waving the note, she added, "This might be my only chance for marriage, short of sitting in the corner and crying 'Heigh-ho for a husband,' as Beatrice said to Claudio."

He paused, and suddenly a touch of color darkened his cheeks. *George Anson, embarrassed?* Outside, the sky had to be falling onto the formal garden and the Hampstead Road. It was certainly a day for firsts, and she wasn't certain how many more strangenesses she could handle before suffering a vaporous, giggling fit.

Finally he cleared his throat. "How precisely do we set about discovering who wrote this atrocity?"

That was more like where she'd initially wanted their conversation to go. Deborah rushed on. "There's the nub of the problem. What excuse can I use for seeing everyone's handwriting? Each person's is different, you know. This is an elegant, plain, honest script, straightforward and perfectly serviceable, but there will be details that give away its author."

"You make it sound like a horse or a table setting, not like an expression of the individual who wrote it." But even as his voice twisted with something more like his usual wry humor, the heightened color faded from his cheeks, leaving a sort of greyish hue beneath his weathered tan. Another strange first. "We could break into all our set's homes at night and sort through their desks and daybooks."

Good old George; he always knew how to make her laugh. To reward him, she did laugh, and hoped it didn't sound too relieved or hysterical. That had been a truly bizarre minute, one she would do well never to repeat. "We could throw a ball, send out invitations, and demand everyone return their answer in their own handwriting.”

“Nah, anyone cunning enough for this stunt would see through that in a flash.” He pushed at the paper, as if he never wished to see it again. “Perhaps you should open a school for wayward dandies.”

For some obscure reason, he seemed to hate her letter, while she wanted to fold it into her book and read it daily for the rest of her life, especially if she ever discovered its author… although perhaps she wouldn’t actually marry him. “What makes you think it’s a dandy?”

“Who else has such good taste in letter composition and materials and yet such a lack of understanding as to morals and deportment? Think of Culver.”

“Good point. You know, you’re right. It is well written, both in handwriting and in the thoughts conveyed. Whoever wrote this has more than a touch of mental elegance.” Deliberately she teased him, unable to resist, and his renewed scowl rewarded her. “And a school—that’s not a bad idea.”

He guffawed. “You think you can open a school?”

“Mama’s literary salon. Everyone secretly wants to be a writer, you know. We invite all our set—all our unmarried set, for if this rascal’s married, then he’ll find no welcome from me—and have Shaw or Anne or even Mama give instruction while everyone writes. And I can wander around the room and peer over their shoulders. We’ll have to invite some women, too, of course, or they’ll think I’m auditioning for a husband…”

The last blood drained from his face, too marked for her not to notice or mention it.

“George, are you quite well?”

He stared, eyes widening. But his pupils contracted as if he were in pain. "Of course. I'm always perfectly well. Why would you ask?"

"You seem... I don't know." Perhaps teasing him hadn't been such a great idea. Certainly it hadn't been a kind one. She'd have to watch that tendency in the future. Playfulness was fine, but cruelty wasn't acceptable. "Anyway, what think you of my idea?"

He shrugged, grimacing. "Might work."

Anson

Might work, indeed. If he participated in her little school, she'd take one look at his scribbles and she'd know—incorrectly, as it happened, but she'd *know*, without a doubt, that he'd written the blasted letter. And then he'd have to be honest, he'd have to tell her he hadn't, she'd think him a liar and a fool— well, certainly the former; she might already believe him to be the latter—and in any case, there would go any chance he'd ever had of catching her challenging eye. Or her affections.

He hadn't suffered such confusion since logic classes at Eton, and there weren't enough forbidden words in the English language to convey his outraged emotions. Too bad he didn't remember the Latin ones. Or the French. Or Greek. Or...

She flipped the paper over, drew her ink bottle closer, and checked the quill's point. "We need an invitation list. Focus on the masculine half first. There's Culver—"

Oh, indeed. "Culver couldn't write that if you held a rapier to his pants."

"Nevertheless." She didn't pause her writing. "Who else? There's Busche—"

"—who's too busy to have written such a note. He'd never have taken the time."

"—but it's just the sort of wooing a busy man might resort to. It's clean, economical, and time-saving. There's Sylvestre Brightenburg—"

From bad to worse. "A pretentious preening fool, not worth the time."

"—but who does an exceptional imitation of Adonis—oh, and Cumberland, of course."

And with the word, the roiling anger in Anson's chest converged into a cold knot of absolute certainty. Only one conniving blighter in all the West End could have pulled off this stunt—Cumberland, the rake, the rich troublemaker, the Scoundrel of Mayfair, the man who'd singlehandedly ruined more gentlewomen than any male should aspire to.

And after ruining them, the rogue had blithely walked away, leaving them to whatever husbands they could find. A civil servant. A linen-draper. A barrister... Not that there was anything actually wrong with Frederick Shaw, Esquire. He was a forthright and honest man. But he couldn't be considered a husband of the first water by anyone beyond his doting wife. Cumberland had left the youngest daughter of a baron for a barrister to pick up.

It had to have been Cumberland. No one else could have possibly dreamed up such a dastardly trick, and with it the blighter had found the perfect way to give Anson a headache. The duke had to still be angry over that ridiculous duel, when Anson had stood second for Rainier. And it just proved that beneath Cumberland's tailored tailcoats beat the heart of a scoundrel. A real gentleman would never stoop to such a low trick.

Question was, what could Anson do about it?

Chapter Four

His Grace

Friday, November 19, 1813

His Grace daydreamed.

It started as a true memory, a memory of an alluring, astonishing young woman, small and slender and straight as a sword, rising on her toes before him and brushing the softest of kisses across his lips. In this memory, her eyes glowed golden-green, her tumbling blond curls draped across one almost-bare shoulder, and her coppery silk gown rustled against his court clothing. The touch of her lips against his turned his insides to molten fire and held him captive, unable to move, to breathe. She'd owned him, body and blood and heart and soul, and he'd loved her.

Then she'd run her finger down his lips, down his chin, his neck, his chest, trailing that glorious, excruciating fire in her wake. She'd stepped back, retreating across the landing of the English staircase, past its white marble Cupids and their bronze lanterns. She'd turned away and vanished around the corner, into the depths of the Dresden Palace, leaving him standing amidst all that elegance, with Godric as usual guarding his back.

She walked away, and he'd charged out to battle and made the worst mistake of his young and foolish life. Because duty had called.

Ah, but such was the power of the imagination that in his thoughts, *she paused at the corner and glanced back, re-igniting the heat within him. Her curls glowed like molten gold in the candlelight. The gown's sleeves drooped off her shoulders, revealing an expanse of exquisite skin that begged for his caress. To hold her, cherish her, protect her from the rampaging army that approached... he could have no higher duty.*

Her first move back toward him was so subtle, it seemed as if she merely breathed. The spell she'd cast held him still, speechless and at her mercy, and only when he again felt the scorching heat of her approaching flame had he truly known she'd changed her mind and returned to his side. His heart pounded, and the fire within him burned in response to hers. When her slender fingers brushed his sleeve, his body blazed beneath her touch, even through the embroidered brocade of his court dress.

"Let me see you to your father." Her rough whisper deepened the spell, and in all the world, nothing existed beyond her. "We've never spoken to our parents... and— and we should—"

"Yes." His voice was hoarse, too. The golden-green of her eyes drew him in ever more deeply. "Yes, we should." He reached for her, and her court-perfect body leaned against his, her arms reaching around him and tightening, her face rising, perfect Cupid's bow lips parting...

His Grace sighed and leaned back in his good English wingback chair. The desk spread before him, scattered with his English correspondence, silver letter knife, a selection of quality quills and inks, expensive wax and a beeswax candle. All to answer a few invitations—the biggest part of his current *English* life.

Tempting though it always was, succumbing to dreams and homesickness would solve nothing. He'd made his choices; he could only live with the consequences. As one of those consequences, not long after he and Godric had arrived in England, almost seven years ago, they had created the persona of His Grace. He'd indulged in the matchmaking game as a sort of camouflage against Napoleon's spies—after all, anyone willing to make such a brazen public spectacle of himself couldn't possibly be taken seriously. Besides, such outlandish behavior gave his honorable father an excuse to disapprove. If Ernst were kidnapped, he'd be less of a weapon in the hands of his father's enemies.

It seemed to have worked, or at least it had been several years since he'd been attacked. He'd never taken a stealthy blade in the back during any of his nighttime strolls through the city, not a successful one, at least. Playing the game—indeed, pretending to be a rake left him free to send information home to his father and little brother, doing what he could from a distance.

A *safe* distance. And that thought rankled more than any other.

His Grace straightened and sipped from the last of his afternoon tea. Cold, of course, since he'd sat and drooled over a beloved memory rather than drink it in a timely manner. The delicate china cup went back into its saucer, and he reached for the next invitation, broke the seal, and began unfolding the paper.

"Another one?"

"Indeed." Godric pushed the salver toward him, the barest curl lifting the corner of his lips.

Ah. The pale blue paper resisted the pressure of his fingers, very much like the single sheet he'd purchased at an out-of-the-way stationer's, as if the respondent hadn't wanted to return a lesser quality than she'd received. His Grace slid the erasing knife beneath the red wax seal, pausing for a second to enjoy the scent of its oil of lavender. Then he unfolded the sheet and read it. And laughed. A literary salon with practice in writing simple love sonnets—of all the clever ideas Deborah Kringle might have adopted, surely that was the cleverest. She'd see each guest's handwriting and glimpse lurking literary talent, if any.

He entered the date and time into his book, then he scribbled a socially acceptable version of "thank you very much, I most certainly shall attend" on the stiff little paper's lower edge. Casually he used his usual handwriting, not the more studied and careful technique he'd cribbed off invitations and notes received from George Anson through the years, prudently stowed in his desk against just such a possibility, along with those of dozens more young *bons vivants*. Oh, learning Anson's style had required some hours of practice, all afternoon of the previous day... time well spent.

A few scrapes from the erasing knife took care of the note's sealing wax, then he refolded the paper and heated the end of his own wax stick, scented with oil of cloves. A dollop dripped in place, stamped with his signet ring, and it was ready to be sent right back to Deborah, lovely young lady that she was.

An excellent move in the game, proving that Deborah most certainly knew how it should be played. But as for the next step—His Grace could only wait to observe Anson's countermove.

Anson

Saturday afternoon, November 20, 1813

His digestion hadn't been the same since he'd read that twaddle-headed letter.

Anson shifted in place, trying to ease the pressure on his neck without touching his clothing. It didn't help his state of mind that his cravat was choking him. Tempting to run a finger beneath his collar, but his valet would murder him if he returned home from Lady Gower's rout with the knot mussed. Why anyone bothered with the silly things... well, it kept him in the highest sort of fashion, and if that helped attract Deborah's attention, then of course it was well worth it.

At the moment, though, she only had eyes and ears for her companions-in-chatter. As a subgroup among the larger and louder group, they formed rather a charming picture, huddled together around Lady Gower's fire. Lissie McTaggart and Violetta de Lisle leaned forward over their teacups, excitement radiating from their shining eyes and eager smiles— lovely lasses, the both of them. They'd been discussing some new maid of honor in the Duchess of Brittany's court-in-exile, but the conversation was now taking a more sinister turn.

It was Chaperone de Lisle, comfortably settled in the center of the sofa with her back well supported, her smile indulgent and her glance amused, who broached the subject. "My dear Deborah, what on earth gave you such an—an unusual idea for an entertainment?"

Anson sniffed into his own cup. What, indeed.

"The dearth of truly excellent love poetry from our younger generation, my lady." Deborah returned her macaroon to her saucer, unbitten. If that lack annoyed her, she didn't allow it to show. "Why, one wonders what they're teaching at our schools in recent years—politics, yes, or architecture, or even law, heaven defend us—but not the important stuff, such as poetry." Her eyes dimmed, presumably at the horrific insensitivity of masculine priorities. "Not love."

Never mind that Frederick Shaw, of their set, was both a writer *and* a barrister. Granted, he wrote Gothic romances, not poetry. Still, the fact remained. But it wouldn't do to contradict her, nor to roll his eyes. Anson contented himself with a sip of tea. A burst of laughter from the card tables, on the other side of the room, distracted him not a whit. He would concentrate on Deborah's conversation to the exclusion of all else. Well, not in case of a fire or alarum. But he'd rescue her first.

"Hear, hear." But Lissie couldn't say that line without a giggle.

And thankfully Deborah hadn't spilled the real reason behind her salon. Playful she most certainly was, but not indiscreet. Not always, at least.

"Unfortunately, Mister Busche had to decline," she pulled a grimace, "but then he's so very busy winning the war, you know. However, he's the only one. Everyone else has responded, and not without some interest in the topic, if I may say so myself." Deborah glanced over her shoulder. Blond curling tendrils draped along the line of her cheek in perfect feathery wisps, and her returning smile morphed to a mischievous grin. "And I cannot wait to see dear George's composition."

As if he were fool enough to allow that to happen. A fool, yes, perhaps sometimes he was, but not to that extent. Besides, she'd neglected to send him an invitation, even though he'd helped her compose the guest list. "Sorry, me girl, I shan't be in attendance. Horrible to miss it and all that, but a previous engagement's in the way."

She froze, her face and shoulder muscles tightening as if he'd threatened to strike her. The brilliance vanished from those blue eyes, and the hurt expression which replaced it was worse than any flinch.

And there went his digestion again.

"Would our delightful company be so kind as to excuse us?" She smiled at the assembled ladies and set her cup on the little table—seemingly oblivious to Lady de Lisle's wide-eyed stare—then rose, grabbed his sleeve in a discreet grip that a blacksmith might have envied, and sauntered casually toward the picture window overlooking the rear courtyard.

Leaving Anson no agreeable option but to follow. And as soon as they were out of earshot—

"But George, I need you there." She released his sleeve and turned at the window, all poise, as if they shared a friendly conversation rather than the tension growing between them. "You're the only one who knows what's going on. Even Mama doesn't know. You must be there to help me."

Well, that little detail, that she trusted him more than her own mother, was flattering, in a strange sort of way. Then again, her bosom buddy wasn't the relationship he'd aimed for.

And this dispiriting little chat... he'd known it was coming, and it hadn't been any help for his innards. There'd never been any doubt that Deborah would be disappointed when he declined her non-invitation. But being hurt by his threatened absence—that he hadn't expected, and a befuddled sort of warm glow lit within his chest. Despite her words, she didn't merely *need* his presence at the literary salon. Judging from her reaction, she *wanted* him there, too. Perhaps...

Outside, heavy grey clouds brooded over the garden. The occasional raindrop spattered against the window, as if the skies couldn't decide what to do, rain or not, any more than he could decide how to handle his dicey situation. The beds lay fallow, a few evergreen bushes holding ranks against autumn but the flowers all in retreat. Not good omens, those.

With their help, though, some common sense returned and routed his warm little glow. Help her, right. Help her onto a wrong track and *perhaps* watch her fancy take off in the wrong man's direction. Or he could let her see his handwriting, blast it all, and then he'd have to stumble through the excuses which would necessarily follow. And oh, would that chat be a lovely one—it would be much worse than this. Really, no, he hadn't written the despicable note—but wished he had.

Something shriveled inside him. When the time for *that* particular chat finally arrived, would he have the nerve to add the final phrase? Could he risk Deborah learning of his... his infatuation? Could he bear her grimace of distaste, of discreetly veiled pity, her turned shoulder, her walk away?

If only he could find an acceptable excuse to avoid her literary salon, something even Deborah couldn't fight. Perhaps he could hire an assassin to murder the old housekeeper on the country estate. Then he'd have to leave and take care of the mess... eh, but he couldn't leave before the Holly Hall Christmas Eve ball. Everybody would be there, and he couldn't miss. Besides, Vicker, his valet, would naturally be upset at the loss of his mother. Truth be told, Anson wouldn't be all that happy over it, either, even if the woman had made his childhood romps that much harder.

No, he was stuck, good and proper.

And confound the man responsible.

"George."

Heaven's angels might know what expressions had crossed his face while he'd brooded. But she'd been watching him every moment—he'd felt her gaze like a pressure against his soul, although he hadn't realized it until the moments had passed—and clearly she'd seen those expressions, too. And whatever they'd been had surprised and puzzled her. Blue eyes wide, vertical creases between her brows, chin drawn back, she looked as if she couldn't believe his reaction.

Come to think of it, neither could he. Had he actually considered murdering his housekeeper? Surely not.

He grimaced, resignation flooding him. If he didn't attend, she'd make certain he received a written invitation for some other made-up entertainment in the near future, and he'd have no choice but to write his response. Whatever he did, someday, somehow, she'd know.

And with his grudging acceptance, it seemed his expression returned to something approaching normal. Her confusion vanished, her face smoothed over, and she straightened with her usual confident, happy smile. "Someday you're going to have to confess to me what thoughts are going through your head in such moments."

No. Just... no. Some things a man had to keep personal or lose his self-respect. "There's not enough oolong in the East India docks for that bribe, and I don't care how much the price rises."

"Well, we'll have to find a better bribe, then, won't we?" Her smile brightened. "Do come, George, please. You always know how to make me laugh and I'll need that. What if my lovely letter was written by someone like Culver or Brightenburg?"

He huffed. "An impossibility, that. They're flash coves, the both of them, without a lick of talent or decency to spare. And if you thought it over, you'd see that I'm right. Sometimes I am right, you know." Not all that often, true.

"Then I promise to think it over... maybe tomorrow." Her grin turned mischievous in a gradual morphing that took a turn or two through appreciation and rue. "Culver's not much, I grant you, but Brightenburg..."

Even though his heart stuttered, he refused to respond to her taunt, not beyond another huff and a glance back to the autumn gardens. Sometimes she knew precisely how to irritate him, as if his emotions had a lever and she had only to switch it to achieve her desired result.

Perhaps he did, at least where she was concerned, and *perhaps* she knew it. And that thought returned him to *someday*, and Deborah smiling at him in a special way, and the mental image that arose had him clasping his hands to prevent reaching for her. In company, well, no, she'd not appreciate *that*. Adoring her in secret was becoming rather more difficult by the day.

"Oh, look! Cumberland's here."

And she left him standing.

A winter freeze jolted through Anson as he watched her return to the group around the fire, which now included the confounded man himself. He clenched his fists as a new and horrible idea occurred to him. Did she know Cumberland had written that love letter? Was her elaborate scheme merely a ploy to bring him out? She couldn't possibly imagine Cumberland, the rake, the Scoundrel of Mayfair, was seriously making a play for her... no, Deborah was smarter than that. But the irony—the man who'd written the love letter was by definition the last man she'd think of.

Beside the fire, in front of Lady de Lisle and the entire assembled company, Cumberland bowed over Deborah's hand as if he meant it. When he straightened, he held on for a second... two... three... until Lady de Lisle's still-widening eyes resembled soup plates rather than mere saucers. The good dame had watched Cumberland's flirtations before; she'd chaperoned Coralie Busche before Rainier brought everything to a head with his ridiculous duel. Surely she'd not tolerate such behavior again, not when she answered to Lady Kringle.

Then Deborah slid her hand free and said something, something inaudible beneath the parlor's chattering guests and the laughter from the card tables. As one, the fireside group glanced Anson's way. And Cumberland... smiled. Or at least his lips curled. But the glint in his eyes, visible even halfway across the large room, couldn't be considered *kindly* by any bewildered sot, much less Mama Anson's little boy. No, that glint leaned more into mocking.

The scoundrel. The shameless scoundrel knew that he knew. And Cumberland knew there was nothing Anson could do but squirm, impaled on the hook.

There, heartburn again. And he'd done nothing to deserve it.

Chapter Five

Godric

Monday morning, November 22, 1813

Godric paused on the predawn street, careful to stand well within the still-deep shadows closest to the storefronts. First light touched Fleet Street's pavement like a tiny candle. Along the sidewalks, where the buildings blocked the awakening day, the street wore a mottled grey cloak, and he hid within it as he waited.

Ahead, George Anson's servant, Vicker, hesitated as well, rotating in a cautious circle and peering all about. His searching gaze passed over Godric's motionless form without reacting, then he knocked on a door, the raps muffled and surprisingly loud in the quiet.

Ah. They'd arrived. The light had fooled him and he hadn't recognized where they were. Godric tiptoed forward. The bookseller's, halfway down the current block, had a recessed doorway, and it made the best hiding place. He ducked into that alcove and waited.

From there, he couldn't overhear the quiet words Vicker spoke to the shop's attendant nor the response, but only the indistinct murmur of their voices. Their tones were light, even bantering, as if

Vicker and the man inside had enjoyed such clandestine meetings before. As of course they had, to Godric's certain knowledge, for it wasn't the first time he'd tailed Vicker in the dawn's early light.

The exchange was short, then the door closed with a quiet thud. Godric backed into the alcove's deepest corner. A flash of movement crossed the opening—Vicker passed the alcove without glancing aside, and then he was gone.

Godric counted to three hundred, giving Vicker plenty of time to get away. Still motionless, he held his position as patiently as if he waited for an enemy sentry to fall asleep at his post. Then he eased from the alcove. A shapeless form openly strode down Fleet Street, already almost to the Strand, and while Godric watched, the form vanished into the grey dimness.

Excellent. Godric hunched his shoulders and turned his toes in—hiding his soldier's bearing—then he walked to the same door and knocked. Within moments, a worker with salt-and-pepper hair answered, wearing an ink-stained apron and peering over a pair of half-glasses.

"Morning," Godric said. He gave his still unmistakably foreign-born voice as much of a local accent as he could manage. "The master forgot sommat important until after Vicker left. He said to say sorry."

The printer's assistant took the folded bit of paper without glancing at it. His Grace had trimmed it from the bottom of an old invitation, received years ago from George Anson, and then he'd written his contribution to the paper on the reverse in the forged handwriting. That way, the feel of the paper wouldn't give the knowledgeable printer reason to pause.

Godric kept his grin a bit goofy. No one would mistake a foolish servant in tattered old clothing with the dignified butler employed at number four,

St. James' Square. And no one would mistake that butler for the former captain of the guard at Dresden Palace, either.

"You tell Vicker that now he owes me *two* pints." A cheerful grin, and the assistant began backing into the shop.

Godric laughed. "Good luck collecting."

Rueful laughter joined his, then the door closed. Godric paused long enough to read the discreet bronze plaque, not yet green with age, beside the door: THE CHATTERER. Then he slid back into the street's shadows and made his way home, keeping a casual eye out for trouble all the way.

His Grace

Tuesday morning, November 23, 1813

The usual furniture in the Holly Hall formal parlor had been moved back against the walls, the sofas and wingbacks arm-to-arm like resting soldiers, and a collection of writing tables and comfortable chairs now clustered about the room's center. The arrangement showed an admirable eye for subtlety, His Grace thought, sitting in one such chair, for while it conveyed all the conveniences of a schoolroom, it didn't give the actual impression of one. A person could return to the role of student for a brief period of time without being reminded too strongly of the fact. For a group of more or less mature adults, at least some of whom had suffered through formal schooling, that seemed like a good, kind thing.

Otherwise the Holly Hall formal parlor retained its casual elegance. The half-height paneling and molding had been polished for the occasion. The lingering scents of beeswax and lemon could mean nothing else, and the dark wood glowed like a line of torches in the morning sunlight blazing through the tall windows and sheer lace drapes. A woman with lesser decorating skills might have been tempted to outfit such a room in yellow or gilt, to emphasize that brilliant light. But the effect would have been overwhelming and would have felt hot, like being inside a square of molten gold. Instead, Lady Kringle, in her wisdom, had selected shades of cool blue with red touches for her décor and the room felt wonderful, stimulating and yet relaxing at the same time.

It was the perfect room for Deborah's literary salon. Her mixed crowd of single young men and women chattered about the tables, fingering the old mother-of-pearl paper knives, the new quills, and small stacks of cut foolscap scattered atop each table, along with the full bottles of ink in red, blue, and green. With such tools, a person could wax poetic in almost any manner desired.

It all created a lively atmosphere for the lesson, and all achieved with merely a new idea and a few simple writing tools. Despite that cost—and the paper alone must have set back someone's pin money for a year—Lady Kringle and Deborah had succeeded in their entertainment before it had even started.

Most entertaining of all, George Anson stalked in at the very latest forgivable moment, stared around the room, stopped when he met His Grace's gaze and bland smile, and then selected a chair as far away as possible.

He himself had been early, of course.

Lady Kringle glided to the front of the room, a picture of elegance in an ivory morning gown with Irish lace. When the golden sunlight hit the fabric, it blazed like a pale candle, drawing all eyes to her. The chattering faded away. At His Grace's table, Miss Lysandra McTaggart and the Honorable Miss

Violetta de Lisle straightened from their huddled gossip session. With such delightful company on either side of him, he had no doubt that his was the best seat in the house.

"Good morning," Lady Kringle said, "and welcome to our first practical literary salon. Before today we've offered lectures and discussions with some of London's finest upcoming writers, but today is something different. Today, we're going to try writing sonnets for ourselves."

Murmurs swept across the room. Miss McTaggart and Miss de Lisle exchanged excited glances and at least one little squeal. Across the room, Anson scowled.

"As you all know, sonnets are love poems of fourteen lines," Lady Kringle continued, "consisting of three quatrains, or groups of four rhyming lines each, plus a couplet at the end that wraps up the poem's central idea or adds an interesting twist. But that's rather a lot to learn in one sitting, especially considering the required iambic pentameter and all that, and not all of us are poetic geniuses, are we?"

Her discreet glance around the room touched on no one in particular. But Anson ruefully popped his eyebrows, as if she'd stared at him alone, and the ripple of laughter from the assembled group contained more sympathy than mirth. His Grace hid his smile. It wouldn't do to smirk, not yet.

"Instead, let's start off with a simple quatrain." Lady Kringle awarded Anson a special sort of smile, warm and kind. Perhaps she'd observed her daughter's attachment, too. "I'll provide the first two lines. You write them down, then see if you can create two more. Remember, the third line must rhyme with the first, and the fourth with the second." She dropped her voice to a conspiratorial murmur. "I have the advantage of you. I prepared my part last evening."

Another ripple of laughter. She smiled again, this time with mischief, waited for the laughter to subside, then closed her eyes and recited from memory. "My love is like the water's raging fall, Full of sound and yearning but no requite." A satisfied sigh. "There. Now write that down and create the next two lines on your own."

A scramble for quills, inks, and blotters, with Miss de Lisle beating out Miss McTaggart for the top sheet and best quill at their table. His Grace joined the fun, scribbling the two lines on the table's last sheet of paper and pausing to think. Rather a Shakespearean beginning, it seemed. With no one at the salon better able to complete the poem than its original authoress, he rather hoped she had. Such a promising couplet would be a shame to waste.

Movement from the corner of his eye, and His Grace abandoned his literary effort, sitting back with an appreciative smile. Beautiful Deborah had arrived, fashionably late and wearing an ivory gown matching her mother's. Tiny wisps of golden curls floated beside her ear, and a small turquoise cross rested on her breast, the same color as the ribbons swept up in her hair. Because she was paler than Lady Kringle, on her the overall effect was cooler, less like a candle and more like a coconut ice.

She paused outside the arrangement of tables and took a deep breath, but something like tension, perhaps excitement, kept her shoulders stiff and her fingers clenched. Then, with a too-casual step, she wandered amongst the student poets, peering over shoulders at foolscaps and handwriting like some elegant variety of study hall monitor. A pause behind Culver and a shake of her head—surely she'd never imagined that lout capable of writing the unsigned love letter. His Grace had thought her more clever than that, but then, she also took the time to stare at

Brightenburg's sheet. Perhaps he'd overestimated her—no, surely not. Surely she just showed caution in checking everyone's handwriting, and she'd gotten the least likely suspects out of the way first.

As she sauntered through the room, greeting her guests and reading their efforts, the tightness in her shoulders and hands increased. Her steps became longer, more graceful. Excitement began glowing from her face, a good complement to the ivory gown, and her mother's eye on her progress remained indulgent, not showing any maternal sort of tension. Deborah hadn't taken Lady Kringle into her confidence, then. And from the innocent glee of the two young ladies sharing his table, His Grace knew they didn't understand the salon's deeper purpose, either. No, if she'd shared her secret with anyone, it had to be…

"George, you're supposed to write it down."

Oh, what fun. And what did it say of the Honorable Miss Kringle that she checked George Anson's handwriting before his? Was she perhaps leaving the most likely for last—and in all modesty came the thought, for hiding the note's authorship remained the biggest risk in his game—or did a stronger interest compel her steps toward her friend? The latter seemed most probable, and he watched her interaction with Anson with relish.

Whatever excuse he mumbled did him no service, for Deborah huffed and planted her hands on her hips. "For pity's sake, George, just write it down." She swept away to the next table and smiled a greeting for the occupants there.

Behind her back, Anson scowled at the inoffensive foolscap in front of him, at the two poetic students sharing his table, at the quill and ink bottle near his hand, and—finally, ultimately—across the room. His Grace smiled in return, aiming for his most cheerful expression and not bothering to hide his unabashed attention. Anson's scowl deepened, and finally he grabbed the quill and bent over the table. A twirl of the pen between his fingers, then he leaned closer and wrote.

No, he didn't *write*. He *printed*, and His Grace chuckled. Trust a sportsman to go down fighting every inch of his doomed way.

"Your grace." Deborah's voice murmured at his shoulder.

He glanced up and rose for her, not finding any hardship at all in extending his smile in her direction. Her gaze lifted from his paper, where he'd scribbled the two lines of Lady Kringle's couplet in his own spiky handwriting, the way he'd write a laundry list or note to himself. It wasn't the rounded, curly version of his cursive that she'd know, the way he'd return an invitation and sign his name. But on the foolscap paper it looked utterly prosaic, without scheme or even much imagination, and he had no doubt she'd just written him off her list of potential love-letter authors.

He bowed over her hand, kissing the air above her glove rather than flirting; he'd already determined such actions would get him nowhere. Granted, even such basic politeness intensified Anson's scowl, visible beyond her elbow across the room.

Her smile in return seemed relieved, which jolted him. *Relieved* that he hadn't written her love letter? In a man, he'd cry insult at such a slight.

"It doesn't seem as if you're finding much inspiration," she said.

It took a moment's thought before he understood her. Ah, of course, she meant that he hadn't attempted to write the next two lines of the quatrain Lady Kringle had assigned.

He leaned closer, conspiratorially, and after a

pause she eased in to match his stance.

"I'm finding the reactions and behavior of your guests so entertaining, the assignment completely slipped my mind." He let his smile twist a bit. Not quite into a smirk, but approaching that territory. "And it would have been a crime not to pause and enjoy your stroll through the room."

She drew back, and for a moment her scowl matched Anson's. Barely even a glint of understanding in her eye, much less delight. No, she had no intention of permitting him a flirtation. "Well, then, consider your attention reminded of it." With a graceful swish of curls and ribbons, she turned to the next table, barely glancing at the efforts of Miss McTaggart and Miss de Lisle.

His Grace laughed and resumed his seat. The two ladies in question shared a puzzled glance, a hint of suspicion in the tightened muscles around Miss McTaggart's eyes—she'd watched him in action before—then they bent again over their foolscap.

It took mere moments for Deborah to finish her initial tour through the tables. Clearly she hadn't found what she sought, for her hostess' smile wavered with disappointment and chagrin. And when she again reached Anson's table, her frustration strengthened. His Grace hid a smile.

"You're not in primary school, George." Her huff could be heard across the room and a furrow appeared between her brows. "I can't believe you printed a couplet. Love poems deserve better." Again she swept away. The furrow, the frown, her tucked chin, all painted a tinge of suspicion atop her deeper emotions. Ah, the path of true love never did run smooth.

Excellent.

Third pass should do the trick. Now to keep the fun from ending too soon.

Chapter Six

Anson

Tuesday morning, November 23, 1813

Trapped. He'd been taken in a wiggle-proof snare and hadn't a hope of escape. Anson growled over his paper, that stupid bit of foolscap that refused to help him at all, that didn't magically sprout Lady Kringle's ridiculous non-rhyme in a handwriting not his own. He really should have studied spellcasting at Eton rather than languages and history and literature and all that stuff he barely remembered. What good was a proper education if it did one no good at all?

More than anything, the confused astonishment growing in Deborah's face told him he was trapped, more surely than a circus barker could. At the thought, something shriveled inside him. He'd disappointed her and that was the last thing he wanted to do. Unfortunately, whatever he did, he'd disappoint her further, and that fried the last of his patience. Cumberland seriously needed a good blasting.

Problem was finding someone who could do it.

And speak of the devil—across the room, Cumberland cleared his throat. His stare fastened on Lady Kringle, resting in a chair in a quiet corner away from the happy, chattering students—silly sods that they were.

Lady Kringle's smile was warm. "Yes, your grace?"

Anson snorted. It was impossible for him to understand why women of all ages found the rake charming. A good blasting, indeed, and preferably a blistering one that reached all his tender places.

"We've not received any instructions on the sonnet's internal rhythm." Cumberland pushed at the paper before him, where two lines—no more; he hadn't written beyond the original offering either—darkened the sheet near the top. The cove had the grace to look embarrassed. "I'm sorry if I'm rushing your planned lessons here, but I'm finding it impossible to go further without a better understanding of what's expected."

One edge of Lady Kringle's smile twisted into something disbelieving and even cynical. Good; she might be charmed, but she wasn't fooled. Cumberland never showed difficulty when bantering literary subjects with Frederick Shaw. Surely he understood sonnets in his bones.

"Yes," Lady Kringle rose, "I had intended leaving meter and the deeper rhyme scheme for a future lesson. But we'll touch on them now, if you like."

And off she went on another lecture. Anson heard the first few sentences and then drifted. Scribbling rhymes, yes, he could manage that, when he wasn't panicking over something as fundamental as his handwriting. But if anyone wanted the rhymes to be *good*, well, there they'd be disappointed.

He had to do something. It was useless, sitting here twisting his innards into lute strings—no good to man, beast, nor sweet angels in heaven. But his options remained as limited as before. He could walk out, insulting Deborah and Lady Kringle and the entire assembled company. He could break his quill, break every silly quill in the room, and brand himself a fool. Well, *more* of a fool, according to the *beau monde*. But no such action would rescue him from Cumberland's trap. Nothing would—

And the paneled doors opened. Footmen trooped in, carrying a buffet table between them, followed by maids with linens, flowers, candlesticks, trays.

Saved by a snack.

Give the sod credit: Cumberland kept the discussion going long enough for the servants to set the table. The spicy scent of cold cuts and the sweetness of fruit perfumed the parlor. Not that he'd be able to eat, but it made a change. Sighing with relief, Anson set aside the quill. Even if the cull merely intended to prolong the agony, well, strange kindness inhabited some cruelties.

And only when he set it aside did Anson realize he'd bent the quill without noticing it. Served the silly thing right for not being magical and getting him out of the scrape.

Food, no, that was beyond his stressed system at the moment. But coffee, yes, that he could manage, that and an overdue question. Anson let everyone else crowd around the buffet, then carried his cup and saucer aside, pushing himself uninvited into the little bit of empty space surrounding Cumberland. He murmured, "You know, if you're still angry over me seconding Rainier, all you had to do was say so. We could have worked something out short of bloodshed."

The sod's sunny, welcoming smile twisted into a feral grin. "But that wouldn't have been nearly as much fun."

He refused to be baited that way. Anson sucked in a deep breath and forced his voice to remain quiet. "Cumberland, old man, why on earth are you doing this?"

Strangely, the smile died. Cumberland paused, the blandness in his expression giving way to—to something completely different, something vulnerable and yearning, and a strange intensity lit him from within. For an unbelievable moment, he looked like another person, younger, more battered by the world but not yet cynical. "Because love should never be denied."

"Love?" Without intending it, his voice rose, more loudly than he'd intended. Still surprised, Anson coughed to cover over his slip. "Who I love, how I love, is none of your business."

"Granted, it's not." The moment passed and the revolting sunny smile returned.

Anson breathed a little sigh of relief. Good. That had been an odd moment, and odd things, things he had to sort out, made his head hurt. Better the devil he knew and all that nonsense. Still... odd barely described it. "So nose out."

"I ask you, precisely how are you intending to force me to do so?"

Silence. Exactly the question Anson had asked himself earlier and hadn't answered. "Well—"

"Do you intend to challenge me?" Again the smile's feral twist. "That worked so well for Rainier."

"I mean—"

"I hear his injury healed well, with barely a scar. You could say he got away lightly."

"Dash it all—"

"Very lightly."

True, that. Unfortunately, all too true. Painfully true. He wasn't a coward, but only a fool invited physical damage with impunity, and usually only a high-minded fool like Rainier. Anson swallowed half a cup of coffee without tasting it. High-minded wasn't generally something even his most admiring friends would say to describe him.

But for the first time, Anson understood Rainier's fury at Cumberland's duplicity, and his willingness to engage in physical combat even knowing in advance it would hurt.

He stalked away, carrying his coffee back to the table. There was nothing he could do. Nothing—

And with a sudden strange clarity, Anson watched, as if from outside his own head, as the thoughts scrambled in there stretched themselves out and finally formed up into a sensible line of reasoning that he could follow. Perhaps it had been Cumberland's casual use of *that word*, the one Anson had been avoiding for close to a year, ever since he'd first spied the Honorable Deborah Kringle wearing a scandalous red gown at last year's Christmas Eve ball. He'd known her casually forever, it seemed, but only at that moment had he glimpsed himself.

He loved her.

Oh, yes, he'd thought in terms of infatuation, of adoring her, catching her, marrying her, a gentlewoman worth the having. But he'd never used that one particular word before, not even in his most private thoughts. Cumberland had thrown it out so casually, as if it were an everyday word like *breakfast* and *blue*, not something special to be treasured and hidden away.

That was the point, wasn't it? He'd hidden it away, and even now, even reconsidering his behavior from this new and startling perspective, he shied from using that word. But he couldn't, not if he truly desired that catch-and-marry business. He'd hidden away his *love* (there, he could use the word in context, too) and he would never draw her mischievous eye like that.

He'd been a coward. He'd hidden his love for her because he couldn't bear to risk it being shattered by exposure, by her rejection. Only by facing his fear and going beyond it could he win her. Only by trying.

Kind of like that five-barred gate over Blenheim way, the terrifying one he'd yearned to gallop around rather than jump over. He'd had to force himself to set Plato to the gate. He'd conquered that gate, but only when he'd hardened his nerve and faced it.

And *perhaps* that had been Cumberland's message all along... the sod.

A shame, the way he'd bent that perfectly serviceable quill, and now it was good only for the fire. Anson grabbed his neighbor's, took a moment with his pen knife to sharpen the point, flipped over the foolscap he'd printed on, and wrote.

Deborah

Something was wrong with George.

It wasn't like him to be so reticent, so—so unplayful and bashful. Not like him at all, and the growl of angry voices from the corner as he'd tangled oh-so-politely with Cumberland had brought a prickly edge into the salon's cheerful atmosphere. Everything had been going so swimmingly until that moment. She'd just known she was only a heartbeat away from identifying her secret suitor, no matter how he'd altered his handwriting—then those two elegant mastodons had clashed and everything had changed. The darkening tension between them was impossible to miss, and throughout the parlor voices lowered, eyes glanced aside.

Had Cumberland written that love note? Was he playing with her, as any rake might, and had George taken such play as an insult? Rumors about Cumberland abounded, everything from grisly tales of feminine conquest followed by casting them aside, to that silliness about him being some sort of foreign prince. As if a prince, foreign or domestic, would hobnob with her and her crowd. As if a prince would stoop to playing such a prank on one of the most minor members of the peerage. It was difficult enough to imagine a *duke* doing so, and yet there he stood, watching her with that outrageous smile.

And yet...

George scowled over his slip of paper, brows lowered in the most forbidding manner. Then it seemed a new thought hit him, rather like a brick, for he froze and his face froze with him. Seconds passed and though he didn't move, she couldn't look away. A voice whispered inside her, insisting upon the moment's vital importance. The anger drained from him, his brow smoothed, and his lips thinned. Finally he straightened, tapped his palms on the tabletop, pushed aside his quill—had he ruined it? the nerve of the man—grabbed another, trimmed it, and then scrawled two lines very fast.

Why her heart pounded, she didn't know. But that interior voice whispered its urgings in a hissing, demanding tone, impossible to ignore. Her feet moved without her permission, sauntering around the outside of the room, sneaking up on him from behind as if intending to steal the hat he currently wasn't wearing, and she peered over his shoulder.

And everything in her life, every preconceived notion and assumption and blithe shred of ignorance—it all vanished in the glance.

Chapter Seven

Tuesday afternoon, November 23, 1813

"George, I had no idea…"

Mama's lesson had ended and the students again scattered around the parlor. Deborah waited until everyone was otherwise engaged with Cook's spice biscuits and tea. Then she cornered George near the window. The tangle of emotions inside her stubbornly refused all her efforts to sort them out, and still she had no idea how she felt about *George* having written her love letter. For love, for romance, she'd expected soaring heights of ecstasy, butterflies in her middle, little explosions of light in her soul, giddiness that transformed her into Juliet. Instead, she was stunned.

George.

George Anson.

He scowled and muttered something incomprehensible, another action not like him at all. In fact, his behavior all day had fit that description, and a thread of confusion twined around her present emotional knot, tying all those bewildered sensations together.

She found more air to speak. "I'm sorry, I didn't

quite…"

With a sudden jerk, he lifted his chin and jutted it out at her. Startled, she sucked in a deeper breath. George only made sudden movements on the cricket field when the ball soared near.

"I know what it looks like." Despite the anger he showed, he kept his voice to a whisper that couldn't be heard at the tea table. "And I don't care. I didn't write that letter."

Which made no sense at all. Her confusion rose higher and a thread of frustration joined it, all those emotions tying themselves into a Gordian knot she'd never untangle. "But I just saw—"

"I *know*." He paused, drew a deep breath, and glanced around the room as if afraid they might be overheard. But even his anger came out in sharp whispers, the soul of discretion. "I know what you saw. Believe me, I've been knowing it for days." Finally he met her gaze. "But I didn't write it."

His eyes. No matter how she felt about him and his behavior, she'd loved his eyes from their very first meeting all those years ago, even during the early days of their acquaintance, when she'd laughed at him along with everyone else. They were a gentle shade like the raw umber her last governess had used in painting, not as deep as even the milkiest chocolate and lighter than his curly hair. Even when he'd been a prancing joke at last year's Christmas Eve ball, his eyes had held her admiration, and not only because of their beautiful color. Even then, she'd noticed their kindness and good humor. It seemed, even when George scowled, his eyes laughed.

Until now, and the emotional tangle in her tummy turned cold and brittle. No, that wasn't fear of being overheard she saw in his eyes, but shame. Embarrassment. Regret. He *had* written the love letter—he had to have. The strong, no-nonsense handwriting she'd seen flow from his quill was too distinctive to mistake. He had written it, but wished he hadn't.

He was ashamed at being caught. George was lying to her. And worst of all—

Anger moved in, setting her tangled emotions afire. She couldn't decide what was worst in such a horrid situation. If he'd simply confessed the joke that first day in the morning room, when she'd shown him the letter, then none of it would have happened and everything would have gone on as before. But with this between them—

Because it hadn't been a very good joke, unlike George's usual fare. And that wasn't like him, either. Which brought her back to her original thought, that something was wrong with George. Well, for now he'd have to sort that out for himself. For now, his poor attempt at humor overwhelmed even their friendship.

Tempting to stalk off with her nose in the air and leave the room in a cloud of silent dignity. But that would leave Mama in the lurch with the entertainment that had been all her own idea. She really did want to, though.

Instead she stalked off with her nose in the air and left George by the window. Violetta and Lissie loitered and munched biscuits near the fire. Instead of leaving the room, she joined them.

His Grace

With a frown, His Grace set aside his cup and saucer. Yes, a step forward in the game. Deborah now had to face her deeper feelings, at least once she recovered from her snit, and George... would be George, still there when she circled back around, still adoring her, still yearning. No, the game progressed, and their disagreement didn't worry him.

But in a quiet corner, unnoticed even by her daughter, Lady Kringle sat without a cup, one uncertain hand hovering near her temple, her head bowed. He could detect no paleness in her face nor shakiness in her hands, and yet... her behavior seemed off.

He gathered a small plate of biscuits of a type he'd seen Lady Kringle enjoy before, fixed a cup to her usual specifications, and headed her way. Time to find out what ailed another beautiful, wonderful woman.

Anson

later that evening

If he'd been Culver, he'd be throwing small things—a bottle of ink, say, or the closest statuette to hand—breaking them and doubtless making a bad situation worse with a colossal mess. Or if he'd been Rainier or Shaw, one of those deep literary-type chaps, he'd be stalking around the room, tearing his hair and likely quoting dire poetry, as if the day hadn't seen enough of the silly stuff already. Fitzwilliam, Caird, the other Celtic types, they'd be spoiling for a fight, and fat lot of good it would do them.

No, he was plain old George Anson, his literary bits weren't deep at all, and his esteemed mama had raised him better than that.

He sat in a comfortable chair, before a comfortable fire, with his feet comfortably up, a brandy beside him and more unhappy thoughts in his head. Even though there was nothing he could do about the situation, still he brooded. Because he was plain old George Anson, of no interest to any young lady worth the having, especially not to *that* one, not now, and there was nothing else he could do. Except perhaps pick that fight with Cumberland... nah, no matter how the sick rage roiled inside him, suicide wasn't in his nature. Only a fool like Rainier picked a fight with a trained soldier. Mama Anson hadn't raised one of those, no matter what the overly educated sorts liked to say about him.

What on earth had he been thinking, to believe that showing Deborah his handwriting would be a good idea? Whatever he'd been thinking, well, he shouldn't have been.

Perhaps he should take himself off to the country. He'd arrive in time for the fox hunting season and Plato was fit, ready for a few gallops... ah, yes, that stirred his blood. A new shotgun wouldn't go amiss and pheasant was always welcome on the table. Rough shooting with the two retrievers...

And he'd wander the woods, shotgun slung and attention lost, shooting too late and frustrating the dogs, because he'd be thinking of the woman left behind in London. She could only be confused by Cumberland's too-clever-by-half actions and his own slow, stilted response. She had to be wondering about him writing that love letter—since clearly it was his handwriting, and he'd not explained himself worth a hoot—and then he'd denied it. Oh, it gave a man a headache and poor digestion, just considering it all.

No, the country was out, not until he'd settled the situation, one way or the other. Not until he had a ring on her finger or a proverbial blade of rejection through his heart.

Perhaps he should just say hang it all and propose to the wood nymph. His situation couldn't get any worse unless she laughed in his face, and surely Deborah wouldn't be so cruel.

Well. Then again, after the day's disaster...

Anson sighed and pushed away the brandy. Getting drunk wouldn't help the situation, either. No, there was only one thing he could do—call on Deborah tomorrow and give her the best explanation of which he was capable. And to achieve that with any measure of success, he had to again sort out his thoughts. Stupid of him not to do that days ago, before he'd let himself be trapped in Cumberland's snare. It sounded like something one of Shaw's Gothic romance characters would do.

A simple explanation. Surely he could manage that without tripping over his blasted tongue. Anson leaned back in his chair and composed himself for serious thought. Not something he did too often, but there... a man could do strange things when backed into a romantic corner.

Love. He loved her. He'd keep saying it, even if only in his head, and set himself to clear her five-barred gate.

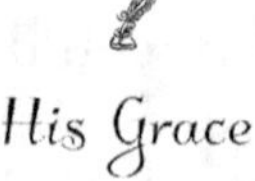

His Grace

Everything felt wrong.

The persona of His Grace could go hang for the evening. He was in; no one should call; Godric was in his rooms with a book; Thomas had the night off; none of the other footmen would disturb him. Alone, he could please himself. Ernst frankly lounged in a high-backed chair, his feet propped on a handy hassock and a brandy decanter and half-full glass near at hand.

Ever since he'd carried tea and biscuits to Lady Kringle, observed her more closely and come to no conclusions regarding her true condition—ever since then, the sensation of wrongness had risen in the back of his mind. By evening, the sensation's strength overwhelmed all his contentment, leaving him with his feet up and working on his second serving of liquid gold, a rare indulgence.

In his conscious mind, he knew the game progressed well and George's move of the day, exposing his handwriting to Deborah, had been nothing short of brilliant. But some deeper, more instinctive part of Ernst fretted. Each successive game he played seemed to push him a bit farther along the spectrum of socially acceptable behavior, making him less of a gentleman and more of the rake he pretended to be.

He'd done nothing more outrageous than walk along darkened, quiet corridors with the lovely Anne Kirkhoven, now Mrs. Frederick Shaw. He'd shared a single kiss with fiery Beryl Wentworth, now Mrs. Finian Fitzwilliam, but it had been behind the bushes in Hyde Park, not the most acceptable of places for the stiff-minded *beau monde*. He'd escorted ethereal Coralie Busche home in a carriage at night, and even though he'd ridden tiger on the footman's seat, he'd left her open to scandal and ruination. Indeed, if it hadn't been for Rainier's challenge, Miss Busche would not now be Mrs. Kenneth Rainier, even though the duel itself had been more farce than tragedy.

The current game… well, little had happened so far. But Ernst couldn't shake the impression that already it had gone too far, that even while he created a new couple within the sight of God and man, at the same time he destroyed something tenuous and precious.

He lifted the glass and sipped, letting the brandy linger on his tongue in all its fiery glory. Strange, but even though he had no idea what his game might be destroying—his morals, perhaps, or his code of ethics—he knew it was nothing he wanted desecrated.

Maybe it was time to give up the game, once the current one finished, of course. It would be worse than outrageous to take Anson and Deborah so far only to abandon them in their confusion. He needed to monitor the situation and ensure that what he'd stirred up became resolved to everyone's satisfaction. But afterward, maybe it was time for his persona to die, as well. His Grace served as protection from French spies, and even after Napoleon's defeat at Leipzig, Ernst had no doubt some diehard *sans-culottes* still roamed London's streets. An assassination attempt or a kidnapping remained disquieting possibilities.

Then again, that was what carriages and large, bruising footmen were for. He and Godric employed six of them, all trained to handle themselves in a fight with fists or swords. He had other means of protection beyond the smug, self-satisfied sneer of a rake.

It would be the ultimate irony to save his body and lose his soul. Once the war concluded and he made his way home to Saxony, neither Ursula nor his father would approve of what he'd become, if he indeed lost his ethics to a game's persona.

So. It was decided. He'd see the current game through to completion. And then he'd let His Grace fade away. He'd introduce his true self, Ernst Anton Oldenburg, first Duke of Cumberland and crown prince of the Kingdom of Saxony, to Mayfair society and all of London.

And may God have mercy upon him, body and soul.

Deborah

The servants had done their duty and once again the formal parlor blazed around her, sunset changing the room's ambiance from molten gold to fire. Deborah lounged in the wingback chair before one tall window, sitting sideways as she'd done when a child, her feet kicking in the air with no one around, thankfully, to see her display of poor manners and immodesty. Funny, how she still thought best in such an odd position. After the day she'd had, it was funny that she could think at all.

So George had played a prank on her. That in itself wasn't particularly unusual. Their friendship had grown more playful and prankish over the last few months, and done so at her own instigation. After all the times she'd yanked off his hat and raced down the street with it, she should have known he'd want payback. But instead of playing his game with him, she'd taken his prank in all seriousness and set out to solve the mystery.

How that must have surprised and vexed him! She'd never seen him so flustered as that morning when she'd first shown him the love letter, the one he'd written himself—not even when he'd been confronted with an obscure literary quotation in ancient Greek.

Normally George would have laughed and admitted the game. But he hadn't, and that she couldn't understand.

Perhaps the answer to his behavior lay in hers.

Why on earth had she taken the joke so seriously? Why had she delighted so in an unsigned love letter? Girls received them all the time, at least in Frederick Shaw's Gothic romances. And when they received one, they always shuddered in distaste, feeding the paper to the fire. Funny how, even in high summer, those girls always had a fire in their rooms.

Then again, no one she knew personally had ever gotten such a love letter. And Shaw was a man. What did he know of the female heart?

For her heart had been tickled. That much was certain. During those few days when she'd carried the secret of her love letter within her, she'd felt so— so flattered, so special. She'd felt light, as if filled with hot air and floating off the balloon's launch pad, and she'd never felt that way before. The newness might have kept her from analyzing her behavior too closely, which in turn might have caused her to panic George with the salon idea and her insistence upon seeing his handwriting. Yes, that seemed right. She'd been surprised and as a result made some poor choices, and as a result of that, she'd backed George into a proverbial corner.

But how could she have known what to do? She'd never been—well, courted seriously before, which in turn was also something of a surprise. As the youngest Kringle daughter, with thirty thousand pounds and *the Honorable* attached to her name, she'd always known she was a good catch, and therefore she'd spurned all casual male advances as an iron-clad rule. Perhaps she'd spurned a few serious ones, too, without realizing it. If she had, they'd been too shy to make their intentions known. No loss there; a shy man held no interest for her.

Short version—she'd never before had a known serious suitor. When one finally had nibbled at her line, even without a signature, she'd leapt to bag him.

Not pretty, what that said about her. It implied that something inside her was desperate for a husband, when the part of her she knew best hadn't even given it a thought. She'd been too busy romping and playing to listen to the rest of her. Had that secret desperation driven her childishness? Had she felt ignored, neglected, bored, and so had romped as a way of catching male attention? Her face heated at the uncomfortable thought. Know yourself, the old Greek sage had said. Harder than it sounded, that.

A husband. Children. Her own household. She held those thoughts in her head and paused, examining her deep internal responses, the ones a girl hardly paid attention to. Moving away from *the dead center of nowhere* would be nice. But if those thoughts aroused anything within her at the gut-deep level, any yearning or excitement, it was too subtle for her to identify.

So it wasn't the generic idea of a husband or even romance which had excited her so. Was it a specific man? Was she secretly in love and not telling herself? Stranger things had happened, at least in Shaw's Gothic romances. If so, who might it be? She tried paging through a few faces in her thoughts. Brightenburg, yes, he was gorgeous, but the shudder he aroused was real. Ditto for Culver, without the resemblance to Adonis.

Maybe someone else. Sir Charles Caird, the Honorable George Ponsonby, Mr. David Crompton... no, she felt nothing beyond a vague inclination toward dancing. Was that how she thought of them, as no more than potential partners? More heat filled her face. They were fellow human beings, not chess pieces on the ballroom floor.

Moving on, then. Cumberland... the name echoed through her thoughts like a battle cry, or a warning. The mystery man who'd escaped the Continent hours ahead of Napoleon's forces, they said, and some of the wisest of her set said he was a foreign prince. Even if that last wasn't true, he was a duke, the first in the current Cumberland creation, and such a glorified title wasn't something to sneeze at. Despite his reputation, his manners delighted... appreciation, yes, she felt that for him, and admiration. Definitely some swooning for his handsome face and proud bearing, as well as a vague sort of competitiveness. But she also felt wariness. She didn't entirely trust him, nor his motives. No, if she was in love, it wasn't with Cumberland.

She huffed out a sigh. There were too many potential suitors in her set for her to consider all of them, one at a time, in a single evening. Already her emotion gauge felt worn out. Odd, but the only sensation she could strongly identify was regret. If she married, she'd have to give up her romps with George.

George.

George.

And Deborah's eyes flew open, a cold certainty congealing around the swooping butterflies in her guts.

There really was a reason she'd found herself staring calf-eyed at him.

Chapter Eight

Deborah

Tuesday evening, November 23, 1813

Deborah stormed from the formal parlor. It wasn't fair. The entire world, the *universe*, simply wasn't fair. Of all the men to fall for... and that wasn't a thought she cared to consider where anyone could see her face. Her rooms... she needed to hide for a while. Maybe forever.

Her slippers *shushed* across the marble floor in the entry hall, and her pale skirts billowed around her as she strode for the stairs. She'd delighted in wearing matching dresses with Mama that morning, thinking in her childishness that she'd find her husband-to-be that day and take those first steps toward the man who loved her. Instead she'd found the worst tangle of her life. George Anson—yes, of course she *liked* him, but...

She gathered her skirts and ran up the stairs.

"Deborah." Her mother's voice came from below and behind her.

Botheration. Tempting to continue and pretend she hadn't heard, but she'd only gotten to the first landing on the sweeping staircase and she stood in full view of the entry hall. Mama had hosted the literary salon for her and deserved better treatment, even if she did insist upon living in the *dead center of nowhere.*

Reluctantly, Deborah paused and turned, glancing toward the staircase's foot as her mother sank in on herself and collapsed into a graceful, unmoving heap on the marble floor.

Deborah

The world bustled around her. Tears trickling down her face, Deborah didn't care and didn't pay much attention, even when Ames sent a footman galloping away for the physician. Her own troubles, her silly thoughts and sillier worries, had faded to a grey fog in her mind, leaving her sprawled on the marble cradling her mother's head in her lap. Terror ate at her soul. Mama was the family's rock. She'd never even had a sniffle before. For her to faint... and that bewildered expression as she'd fallen, as if she hadn't understood what was happening to her.

Unbearable. Deborah leaned over and kissed Mama's forehead, a delicate, lingering touch. At least she still felt warm, not waxy or anything horrible.

"Miss Deborah."

She glanced up. Ames crouched beside her, compassion on his usually inscrutable face. Behind him, two burly footmen held a paneled door, removed from its hinges. It looked like the one from the pantry.

For a moment she blinked with confusion. But of course they had to carry Mama upstairs and get her comfortable before the physician arrived. Deborah leaned back out of the way, and they set the door on the marble beside the motionless form.

Ames slid his hands beneath Mama's shoulders and lifted. She hardly noticed the discreet brush of his hands against her thighs. Barely a breath had Mama taken, and Deborah's heart squeezed itself into a painful, cold ball, tighter with every second.

No, there—a flicker of eyelids. "Mama?"

And *there*, her eyes opened, lids fluttering like a frightened butterfly's wings. Mama glanced around, at Ames bending near and supporting her weight, at the footmen, appropriately enough at her feet, at the ceiling overhead and the newel post looming beyond Ames. Confused lines furrowed her brow, as if she couldn't understand how she'd gotten down on the floor.

Then the confusion faded, and Mama's usual fire returned. She lifted one hand. Hope flaring, Deborah reached for it. But Mama grabbed her wrist with a grip like a dockman's, and when those eyes finally cut to her—last of all she looked at her daughter, she'd examined the *staircase* before her— the steel in Mama's eyes matched her grip.

"Don't you DARE try to cancel the ball."

Don't— Don't try—

Baffled, Deborah swallowed. Then Ames and the footmen together swung their patient onto the door, lifted it, and carried her away.

Still joined, their arms stretched across the growing distance, Mama hanging on with that dockman's grip until it seemed she'd drag Deborah upstairs with her. Then the steel in her eyes faded to fear and she let go, dry fingers stroking the back of Deborah's hand in passing, a gentle touch more like a mother's. The footmen hefted their burden higher, Ames carried his lower and backed up the stairs, keeping the door and its sad burden level as they disappeared above the landing.

Help. She needed help, someone to talk to,

someone who'd give her advice and calm her soul. She needed George—no, not with her unsettled, uncomfortable feelings, not with that dead certainty that still weighed like lead in her stomach. If they hadn't argued, she could send him a note, saying she was at home and hinting for his presence. He would never refuse such a subtle invitation. But after the stupid salon...

No.

Instead she waited on the bottom step for the clattering rush of the carriage, returning in a mad dash, and escorted the physician in his old-fashioned black coat and powdered wig to Mama's bedchamber. She hovered alone at the bedside, watching Mama's still form as he examined her, and overheard Ames saying he'd sent to the country for Papa. She hadn't even thought of him. It was a good thing the servants ran the place and not her. She'd have left the poor man none the wiser. And something inside her seemed to shrivel away as the examination went on, and on, and on.

Finally, when she knew she could bear it no longer, when she had to learn the facts or scream with madness—finally the physician straightened, a kind little smile on his face.

"I assure you, my dear Lady Kringle, you're in no danger. A rest and a tonic should set you to rights. Again you've done too much, worked too hard, taken too many tasks upon yourself—"

He kept going. But Deborah heard no more. Guilt swam in with his words like a rushing tide, overwhelming her diminishing fear. George had told her she should have been helping Mama organize the ball. She'd laughed at him for that, as she'd laughed at him for almost everything he said.

But he'd been right. She should have been helping. She hadn't, and Mama's illness was her fault.

Deborah

Wednesday morning, November 24, 1813

"My dear, I have a shameful confession to make."

If anything shamed Papa, Deborah could detect no sign of it, for he leaned back in the chair with his usual serene expression. He'd arrived in time for breakfast after traveling all night, and couldn't seem to understand why she'd exclaimed over highwaymen. So maybe highwaymen no longer operated in the areas between town and the country estate. Maybe she was overreacting. But it was bad enough having one parent at risk, and it seemed selfish of him to have risked himself, too.

Outside, showers pattered against the morning room window in fits and starts. Little light made it through to her table. The bit of paper she'd pulled forward, intending to write a note to George after all, lay in shadow. She wished she could hide, too, and never receive unsigned love letters that started such awful trains of events into motion.

Was Papa awaiting her response? "Shameful." Though she said the word, still she saw no evidence of it in his expression.

He at least had the grace to shift in his chair. "Indeed. Your mother and I argued on Friday last—" he had to mean via their daily letters to each other "—and we haven't spoken since."

That made her pause and widen her eyes. But when she thought back, she couldn't recall Mama sitting at her desk writing her letter to Papa yesterday morning. Nor the day before. How had she missed that? As usual, Mama's elegant carved writing desk, tucked beneath the next window over, gleamed with polish and looked as if no one had ever marred it with ink or battering chairs. Which was decidedly unfair, considering how much Mama used it. Some people had such a light touch with the furniture, and then there were people like her... and her mind was wandering.

She shook herself. "So if Mama felt ill—"

His brows furrowed and he bowed his head. "—then I knew nothing about it, either." He reached across the table and laid a gentle hand on her wrist, the one Mama had gripped so tightly. "And therefore you have no more reason to feel guilty than I."

"You weren't living in the same house with her." Deborah slid her fingers into his. No matter what age she reached, the simple touch of her father's hand could solve anything.

Except this. And *not speaking...* that sounded horribly familiar and not like anything she should be doing. Poor George; were they not speaking? Whether they were or not, she owed him a note and an in-person apology for treating him so shabbily and for taking his joke too far. They'd been comfortable friends, but she'd made a hash of it and he deserved better.

"Perhaps I should have been living in the same house with her. And then perhaps I would have seen her condition for myself." Papa squeezed Deborah's fingers and rose, releasing her and tugging his morning coat into position over his spare frame. Some men put on weight as they stretched into middle age; not Papa, despite the surname of *Kringle* his parents had chosen and heaped upon him. Father Christmas he definitely was not. "Somewhere in that desk of hers, your mother keeps a book with a sort of permanent guest list. But it will need tweaking before the ball's invitations are prepared. It always does."

And with that casual bombshell, he ambled away.

Deborah stared at his back as he vanished beyond the doorway. Ice trickled through her and prickles stung her hands. *Mama gripping her wrist like a dockworker; steel in her eyes. "Don't you DARE try to cancel the ball."*

Of course Papa didn't organize social events. He couldn't always even be counted on to attend them. He never did that sort of chore himself. Mama had always handled the entertaining, both as hosts and guests, and she'd made the Christmas Eve ball her own. But what he'd said— He couldn't possibly intend for *her*—

A cold knot of terror tightened her stomach. Deborah shivered.

He did. And so did Mama. They wanted her to manage this year's Christmas Eve ball.

Panic followed. Of all the extended Kringle tribe, she was the least organized, the least mature, the one least likely to succeed at such a venture. The task should go to the eldest daughter, or even the eldest son; sauce for the goose and all that. Merely because she was the last one at home, on the premises and handy for the grabbing—

George. She needed help, someone to calm her and help her sort out the situation, and that meant George. But the bit of paper waiting before her, the one she'd mentally covered with the necessary invitation, remained stubbornly blank, and the tone she'd earlier decided upon now seemed utterly wrong. Too ordinary, too careless. Too flippant, just like her behavior before Mama's collapse. She'd intended only a friendly note, but then to break such news to him upon his arrival? No, that would be a horrible way to treat anyone, much less such a good friend as George.

Did she lean on George's comforting presence so much? The evening before, with Mama being carried up the stairs, her first thought had been to send for him, even before she'd considered Papa and his much closer claim. Now that she'd been presented with the monstrous task of organizing the Christmas Eve ball, she found that again, her thoughts turned to George. And there, a gentle warmth seeped through her cold bones as she imagined him sitting across from her—

"Miss Deborah."

The cook stood in the doorway, black slate in hand and round frame heaving a bit, as if she'd run up the stairs. She bobbed a curtsey.

Ah, the menu for the week, a customary planning event between the cook and the lady of the house. A little chore like that was something she could handle, and Deborah managed a smile. "Yes, Mrs. Dunavent?"

Cook advanced a few steps into the morning room, as if afraid of being trapped there. "I need instructions for the Christmas puddings, miss, the ones for the big ball."

The warmth that thoughts of George had inspired died beneath another rush of chills. "Perhaps you should wait and ask Mama when she recovers."

The cook paused in the middle of another cautious step, her eyes rounding to match her face and the rest of her. "We can't wait any longer, miss. Stir-Up Sunday's in four days and I must let the grocer know the weights if we expect to get everything in time."

If it was a conspiracy against her, the cook was in on it. "But how would I know—"

"Miss Deborah?" Ames appeared in the doorway behind Mrs. Dunavent. "We should discuss the dining arrangements for the Christmas Eve ball. We'll need to pull the larger tables from storage and clean them, and of course the best plates and silver and linens." He paused, kind eyes examining what had to be the bewildered terror on her face. His businesslike voice softened to spoken honey. "The number drawn from storage depends upon the invitation list, you know."

A conspiracy, yes, it had to be. For the housekeeper appeared behind Ames, and she could only want to discuss the extra help needed for the occasion. She had that need-to-know-now expression on her face, the same one Ames wore, the one she hadn't initially recognized on Mrs. Dunavent. The cold spread through every fiber of her body, even her littlest toe.

When the housekeeper opened her mouth, Deborah raised a hand. "A moment, Mrs. Ames." Astonishing that her teeth didn't chatter. "All of you work closely with Mama. Did you know she was ill?"

Glances between them told her all she needed to know, and anger moved in behind the cold fear.

Ames cleared his throat. "She ordered us to keep her secrets, miss, but yes, she's claimed to feel poorly for several days now."

"Last Sunday," the cook said. "After dinner, when she'd normally answer invitations and letters, she rested in her rooms instead."

And there it was, the clue she'd missed. Before she could think on it, Mrs. Ames chimed in. "She didn't wish to worry you, miss, nor the Lord Kringle."

Hard to fault them for obeying orders. And there, in the three senior servants, lords of their own domains, stood the answer to the terror that swamped her. "Lord forbid there be a next time—"

Exclamations, and an echoed "Lord forbid!" from Mrs. Dunavent.

"—but it seems clear someone should have gotten help for her before the crisis point was reached. Should Mama ever again feel poorly and I be too stupid to notice, of your kindness, you will inform me."

More glances. And finally, slow nods. "Yes, miss."

"As for your questions," and with her glance, she included all three of the senior servants, "do whatever worked last year. It's not only Mama's guidance that makes the Christmas Eve ball the event of the season. It's your own experience and efficiency. That's our biggest advantage and if we're not to ruin the ball before it begins, we must use it. Mrs. Dunavent, for the puddings, your clear head will guide you. My only suggestion is to order heavier weights for all the ingredients, rather than lighter. It's better to be prepared for too many guests than too few, and any leftovers can be given to the orphan's school." The poor orphans down the road were the only people closer to the *dead center of nowhere* than Holly Hall.

As they filed out, Deborah rose from her little table and the still unmarked scrap of paper. George's letter had to wait, much as she yearned for his company and strength. She also yearned to avoid the heavy task settling over her shoulders. But it was impossible to contemplate failing Mama, not with her upstairs lying ill, no matter the physician's soothing words. If Mama refused to let her cancel the ball, and if that meant she had to organize the entire event herself—well, then, she'd better get started, no matter the freezing in her limbs.

No matter that she had no clue where to start.

With a sense of sacrilege, of turning some corner in her life she'd far rather avoid, she crossed the morning room to Mama's desk and eased down into the carved walnut chair. It seemed an invasion. Everything was so orderly, quills in the holder, paper knife and pen knife and scented candle arranged just so, paper on its shelf, ink bottles on another. Turn *her* loose in such an organized space, and she'd wreck it inside an hour. She'd have to be careful and remember where everything went.

In a vertical slot stood Mama's book of hours, her journal, the accounts ledger, and the household management book. The latter seemed most likely to hold a permanent invitation list, and Deborah eased it from its place with cautious fingers. From beyond the door came a murmur of voices, the senior servants exchanging their thoughts as they moved away. Strange, they didn't sound worried. Indeed, that last note, as their voices faded down the stairs, sounded suspiciously like a giggle.

Her face heated, melting the ice in her veins. They expected her to fail. If she'd been forced to lay down her pin money on the question herself, she'd have been strongly tempted to back their opinion.

She really needed George.

Chapter Nine

Wednesday morning, November 24, 1813

Buttered eggs yet again. Considering all the eggs he'd been eating lately... somewhere, in some poultry yard nearby, the hens were happy and productive. Anson set that morning's edition of the *Chatterer* beside his empty plate, loaded said plate appropriately for what could only be another difficult day—he had to deliver his apology to Deborah and learn the gentle art of wooing—and settled back while Sandringham poured a first cup of tea.

Despite the day's potential terrors, it was hard to feel upset when faced with buttered eggs and morning's liquid gold restorative. Anson put away his worries and trials, sighed with satisfaction, lifted his tea, and took a sip, while raising the paper for the first glance.

The tea went down the wrong way and burned a scalding path along places tea had never been intended to go. By instinct Anson snorted, sending it up behind his nose into more places ditto. Coughing took him and he choked, spilling the remainder all over his plate, pants, and what looked like the best Irish linen tablecloth, the one with the fancy lace insets, the nearest lace now stained a delicate and spreading brown.

Yet he couldn't bring himself to care, not when he stared again at the *Chatterer* and re-read the line that caused the domestic disaster in the first place. Furious heat scorched Anson's entire body, not only the spot on his thigh where the tea had burned him before starting its drip to the floor.

Another incident. Another, and it placed Cumberland's behavior well beyond the *scoundrel* level and ripped straight through the register to *utter cad*. And if he thought he'd survive the encounter, Anson would now cheerfully call the blistering cove out in a heartbeat. Pistols at dawn—with those he might stand a chance.

Deborah

She couldn't show Mama her fears, not with the poor woman lying on what could prove to be her deathbed despite the physician's soothing words. No, she had to show a brave, cheerful, confident face. But her heart over-shouted her thoughts and pounded a slow and dreadful beat in her chest.

Deborah paused on the threshold and treated her interior anatomy to several deep breaths. Her old governess, the one who'd planned to live at least to ninety, had recommended that, and she'd instructed Deborah to imagine all the good little bits of air swimming through her body and strengthening her for the trials to come. It was time to find out if the silly woman had been right after all.

Face appropriately schooled, Deborah pushed open the paneled bedroom door and slipped in, fully expecting to find the invalid collapsed back among her pillows with a wan face and trembling hands. What she actually saw jolted her to a stop.

She certainly hadn't expected to find Mama sitting up in bed, propped against the headboard, book open atop a pillow in her lap and a steaming teacup beside empty breakfast dishes on the mattress beside her.

Relief rushed through Deborah, and she released the used air she'd held in her lungs for too long. Mama's little smile seemed tired, yes, and the tiny lines beside her eyes deeper than normal. But her color was excellent, her hand on the page steady, and the windows gaped wide open, pale sunshine bathing her with a hint of gold. If the physician had been at all concerned for her safety and simply not admitting it, the windows would have been shut tight against drafts. So he'd spoken the truth—Mama was in no danger, and everything could return to normal in a few days.

The relief soothed Deborah far more than the air had. But guilt followed behind it. Was she more worried for Mama's health or for her own sanity, with the task of organizing the ball hanging over her head like that sword in the old Greek myth? For if Mama truly was well, then she could resume the task herself as soon as she'd rested. Deborah would cheerfully give it up without a single regret.

The pause while she'd stared and thought had dragged on for too long, and who knew what expressions had illustrated those thoughts across her face? Whatever they'd been, they'd been observed in their passing. Those tiny lines beside Mama's eyes crinkled as her smile grew, and the eyes themselves narrowed with mischief. As if in response, the sunshine around her brightened. Deborah couldn't stop it; she smiled back. It was a beautiful and heartening picture.

Perhaps too beautiful for the stated situation.

And simply as that, a thread of suspicion joined her guilt-tinged relief. That dramatic collapse at the foot of the stairs had been rather... *conveniently* timed, had it not? At precisely the moment when the ball's preparations could wait no longer, when chatter in the drawing room would no longer cut it and the great train of events had to be started—that was the moment Mama had called her name and collapsed in plain sight, falling to the foyer's marble and earning nary a bruise on her tender limbs. Granted, she'd shown symptoms for days before—if the servants could be believed. If they weren't all conspiring against her. Or if Mama hadn't played a role and let them believe the skimpy evidence she'd displayed.

No, surely not. Surely she maligned her own dear mother. Yet the idea, once allowed into her thoughts, refused to leave them.

"It's good to see you up, Mama." She'd ignore that unfounded suspicion and remain soothing and cheerful. Deborah sucked in more good air and bustled around the bed, smoothing the covers, feeling those sharp, perceptive eyes boring into her with every movement. She'd ignore the heat building in her face, too.

"It's good to *be* up. Work might be tiring, but sickness is no fun at all." Mama stretched like a cat and leaned forward. Taking the hint, Deborah restacked the pillows behind her, tucking the little one into the curve of her spine. The luxurious sigh as Mama leaned back spoke to how well she'd performed the task. "Oh, that's good. Thank you, my sweet daughter."

A tug settled the snood into a more comfortable position behind Mama's ears, then Deborah bustled back around the bed. She could clear the breakfast things while they chatted, then leave the poor woman to rest in peace. She would not entertain that horrid suspicion, not for a moment longer, no matter how sharp the eyes drilling into her nor how self-conscious the blood still warming her cheeks. And she most certainly would not ask the question burning in her soul: how soon Mama could resume her accustomed duties.

Including that despicable ball. Honestly, Deborah's only interest in the event were the gowns, the potential partners, and the dancing. Organizing it was no fit chore for someone as lacking in skills as herself.

But she could ask a more general question. "Presumably this healthy image you present means you feel much better and you'll soon be ready to return downstairs to your lonely daughter?"

"Well."

With the word, Deborah's heart quit its job and stopped beating entirely. Her hand lifting the plate stilled, too.

"Better, yes." Mama retrieved her cup with a perfectly steady hand and sipped. Tea—the physician had approved her for tea. No worries about her being overly stimulated, then. Would he permit strong oolong for a patient whose condition worried him? Weak tea, willow bark, or chamomile, absolutely, but not a beverage with that deep, enticing color. And would an overly-tired woman of a certain age recover quite that swiftly?

Without Deborah's permission, the thread of suspicion in her soul strengthened.

"Indeed yes, I do feel better." The cup returned to the saucer, and Mama to her pillows. But her hand's weak little flop onto the coverlet didn't seem quite believable.

Or maybe she herself was imagining things that

weren't there. Deborah shook herself and straightened, setting the cutlery and napkin atop the dirty plate. The situation would be so much simpler if someone provided her with a guidebook to understanding sickroom symptoms… or the lack of them.

"But not fully recovered, and I don't believe I'll be ready to return downstairs for some time yet." The golden glow around Mama winked out, as if a cloud wandered past and blocked the sun. But before it vanished, Deborah got a good look at her face. Not a hint of paleness showed, nothing wan or sickly about it. "Hopefully that won't interfere with your own plans? How are the arrangements for the ball proceeding?"

Deborah froze. Suspicion died. Certainty solidified, and slamming the breakfast things back down and abandoning the resulting clutter wherever it fell seemed an appropriate response. But that would be ill-mannered, even if it did feel justified.

Mama ill? She no longer believed it. Mama forcing Deborah to organize the Christmas Eve ball for nefarious reasons of her own? All her pin money would back that bet, and she hated to lose.

She'd been set up, not once, but twice—and by those closest to her. Once by George with his silly joke of a love letter, and then by her own mother's pretended collapse. And like the simplest Reuben from the country, she'd swallowed both, hook, line, and sinker.

Chapter Ten

Anson

Wednesday morning, November 24, 1813

So many times he'd arrived at Holly Hall for a visit, tossing Plato's reins to the groom, pausing to admire the imposing façade, and wondering about those silly statues. The most memorable time had been his very first visit calling specifically on Deborah, rather than the family—Boxing Day, that had been, two days after last year's Christmas Eve ball, and he'd been so nervous, her so funny and kind. It took no effort at all to remember her startled expression when the butler had announced him, then the swiftness with which she'd produced a welcoming smile. An after-dancing call on a gentlewoman was perfectly ordinary and expected by society, but in her kindness, she'd acted as if she'd never had such an honor before. Such giddy emotions had swirled through him. He must have been in love with her already and not even known it.

He climbed the steps and rang the bell. Ames welcomed him, as inscrutable as ever, and escorted him through the graceful mansion. Anson followed, uncomfortably aware of the unusual thumping of his heart. It was impossible to expect such kindness now, after their misunderstanding at the literary salon when he'd bungled his lines so badly. No, he could only expect a frown and a scolding, especially when he brought out the *Chatterer* and showed her how they'd been played. She'd romped with him up and down Fleet Street, but he'd never cast a shadow over her reputation. Not a real one, at least, not anything that their set would take seriously.

At the upstairs landing, Anson paused and sucked in a deep breath. Their friendship couldn't go back to the way it had been. He'd apologize, and he would court her. And if she laughed in his face, he'd at least have his answer. But it was time to leave *perhaps* and *someday* in the past.

And there, as the morning room opened before him, he spied her little table beneath the window, the wan autumn sunlight falling on a stray scrap of pale blue paper, the sort she used for sending invitations. But her chair sat empty. Well, at this mid-morning hour, she might be otherwise engaged. Ames would call her and he would sit quietly waiting, and not prowl all over the room as if he'd lost his mind. Granted, it felt as if he had, but still, he could show some manners.

Ames paused in the doorway, blocking his view. "Mister George Anson, miss."

Wait, over there—she worked at Lady Kringle's carved walnut writing desk at the second window. Strange, that, and his heart thumped even harder. Deborah avoided her mother's work space like the plague, as if she feared Lady Kringle's maturity and capability were catching. For her to sit there...

Something had happened.

And as the thought flashed through his mind, she shot from the chair like pellets from a shotgun, whirled, strode across the room... and froze, staring at him over the butler's shoulder. She stood svelte and beautiful as ever, like the wood nymph he fancied her, and those sudden angry movements emphasized her grace—never a stumble or bobble, just pure perfect motion. Her frumpy old pink morning gown needed to be ripped up for rags and flyaway wisps of golden hair abandoned her quick and dirty bun in droves. He'd never seen a woman more lovely, more desirable, and if he didn't catch his breath, his heart might stop.

No one so wonderful could ever return the affection of someone so blatantly ordinary as him. And if she was *that* angry... maybe he should run for it.

Quick as that, his courage and determination deserted him. A small panic shivered across his skin. He needed to rethink his plan. And with the thought, despair joined the mix. Oh, yes, thinking always worked out *so well* for him.

"George." She finished crossing the room, her hands reaching. Ames somehow melted away from between them and when next Anson blinked, he sat on the sofa, Deborah on the chair across from him. Her lips moved, but no words came forth.

No, she wasn't angry, or at least not angry at him. At closer range, the tightness around her eyes and her pinched mouth seemed more anxious, even frightened. The quiet expression in her eyes hinted at...

Gratitude?

His first instinct had been right. Something *had* happened, something bad.

Without waiting to think further, he leaned into the space between them. "What's wrong, my dear?"

Deborah

"It's Mama." Deborah couldn't stop the rush of

words. They insisted upon being said, and she could only get out of their way. "She collapsed last night at the foot of the stairs." Then, when George's eyes bulged and he blanched, sucking in a deep breath, she hurried on, more deliberately. "The physician assures us she's in no danger, that she merely needs rest."

His beautiful brown eyes eased back to their more accustomed size, but he remained leaning toward her, as if he sought to comfort her with his physical presence. "Still, what a horrible shock for you."

"Frightening, yes. Mama's never been sick, not a day to my knowledge." Oh, if only she dared reach across and seek his hands again. That touch, while he'd let her drag him to the sofa, had tingled her fingers and shivered her toes. Comforting, yes, his physical presence and touch comforted her, and yet it did more than that, in a strange way she couldn't quite define. Some... *interesting* new sensation danced along her hands, making her quivery and yearning for his repeated touch.

But she didn't quite dare reach for him. If he should pat her hand like an elder brother or friend, and set her hand aside—she'd die on the spot, right where she sat. Would he? Good-natured, kind, and forgiving, George acted as if nothing had happened between them, and with a rush of gratitude, Deborah accepted his implied offer. If he could shrug off their misunderstanding and the tension which had followed, so could she, and their friendship could return to the easiness it had always known. And those silly romantic notions swimming around in her heart she would ignore, no matter how they squeezed at her and no matter the ache ignoring them brought forth.

She swallowed and continued. "And you know,

this morning, she took breakfast, and tea, and her color seemed very good, not pale or sickly at all." It was strange, the amount of effort required to piece two coherent thoughts together. "So even though I've been wild with worry, even I must confess the physician seems to have told us true."

"Well, that's good news, at least." But dear George remained pale, as if her words hadn't quieted his fears.

In a rush, Deborah decided to tell him of her suspicions. "In fact, I'm even beginning to wonder..." She paused. If George disagreed with her assumptions, then she might never live down those suspicions—and in another rush, she realized she didn't care. If he wanted to tease her mercilessly for the remainder of their lives, and even haunt her into the afterlife, it would be worth it to have his steadier opinion. "I'm beginning to wonder if she is ill at all."

His brows swooped up toward his hairline. "Because she took breakfast and her color is good?"

"Because Mama has never been ill, but now she requires several weeks in bed, leaving me to manage without her." She grimaced. "It's difficult to put into words. I can't point to a single action or statement she's made that created these suspicions in my heart. Nevertheless, after seeing her this morning, I cannot rid myself of the thought that I'm being played."

His beautiful eyes turned somber, his brows returned to their normal position on his forehead, and he leaned back a few inches. For a moment, Deborah almost reached for his hands to draw him back. Then she came to her senses and clasped her hands in her lap.

"Sharp as you are," he said, "if your dear mama attempted to fool you, I doubt if she'd succeed."

Warmth flooded through her. Deborah leaned

into the space he'd vacated, eager to discuss the subject in depth... but then she paused. No, the conversation had centered upon her and her troubles for long enough. He seemed agitated, and as hostess and friend, it was her office to tend his needs. "George, is everything quite all right?"

He paused, flattened his lips, then yanked a folded newspaper from his pocket and thrust it at her.

What on earth? She accepted it from his hand, restraining the urge to touch his again in passing—*just as an experiment,* the unhelpful part of her whispered, *to examine that interesting sensation again*—and she turned the paper around for reading. The latest *Chatterer,* it was, and with a fat and angry pencil someone had circled a few sentences... which detailed the beautiful love letter the Honorable Mr. G.A. of Mayfair had written to the Honorable Miss D.K. of the Hampstead Road, even if he hadn't had the nerve to sign his name to it.

Strange, how she'd forgotten her love letter, except as the catalyst that had wrecked her friendship with George. Since Mama's collapse, she had not considered that swooping, floating, elated feeling the letter had originally caused. And yet here it came again in all its wild glory, a thrill that left her innards dancing like fairies around a toadstool. With a smile, she set the *Chatterer* aside. "It doesn't matter."

His mouth twisted into a grimace. "Deborah, my dear, you must understand." He paused, staring at his hands, as if gathering his thoughts, or perhaps his courage.

That was the second time he'd called her *my dear,* a phrase he didn't usually indulge. Sudden hope stirred in her chest, cutting through the letter's lingering thrill. Might he... did he feel for her as she did for him? But as suddenly as the hope arose, it also died. No, that was clearly impossible. His behavior hadn't changed, and one thing all the romances, Gothic or otherwise, agreed upon was that when a man fell in love, his behavior became adoring and protective, that he couldn't bear to be apart from his beloved, that his entire world began revolving around her. George showed no sign of any such change. Indeed, her first impression had been correct. He wanted their friendship to resume and continue as before... as friends.

And that was a desire she could no longer share. But for him she'd pretend, since clearly it meant so much to him.

Finally his gaze rose and met hers. Some hot emotion glowed from his beautiful brown eyes. "I didn't write that letter."

He said the blunt words and stared at her, an expression of such frank earnestness on his face that she could think of nothing to say in return. His face... had she ever thought him plain or doltish? The clean, sloping lines of his cheekbones, those swooping brows and dashing devil-may-care lips, his sportsman's strong coloring and the weathering of his skin... she clasped her hands again rather than reach for a sampling. Heat building in her face, she looked away.

George never lied, and it was impossible to believe he did so now, with his heart so plainly visible on his face. Heavy guilt swamped the flutters tightening her stomach. She'd abused him with the very thought. No, someone had set him up, and when she discovered the culprit, she'd feed him some bitter medicine indeed.

But the glance aside fell on Mama's desk, the chair pushed away to where she'd left it and the household management book open to the midpoint.

Beside it lay a scrap of paper scrounged from some-where, a quill, and the poor desk's first ink splatter, forever enshrined as a testament to her clumsiness. She'd been making frantic notes when Ames had announced George, and she'd dropped the quill in her haste.

The sight wiped even the guilt and cold anger from her mind. In Mama's book she'd found a sort of timeline, detailing what needed to be done by when if the Christmas Eve ball were to run smoothly. Her initial guess, earlier that morning, had been correct. Nothing had been done, and minutes ago she'd been scribbling out the day's tasks before dressing for a mad dash to town. Much as she wanted to stay and sort things out with George, she couldn't.

Angry at Mama—yes, she was, and payback was going to be glorious. But the consequences of the ball being a failure, which it would be if she didn't do her enforced part, were too scandalous to even consider. She had to play the part assigned her, like it or not, and for now, that meant George, and all the fascinating emotions and sensations he aroused within her, had to wait.

"I believe you," she said, and swallowed the joke—*with that poetic style? if I'd thought about it at all clearly, as you'd urged me to...*—which normally would have followed. Their friendship couldn't re-turn quite to its relaxed status, for she'd never be able to make mean jokes about him again. The thought was both comforting and bittersweet. "But there's something else. Mama's devious plan of tak-ing to her bed for the next few weeks leaves me in charge of organizing the Christmas Eve ball. I found some instructions—" she waved at the book, still open on Mama's desk beside the brand new ink splat "—but there's so much to do." A deep breath, and she said the hardest words she'd ever attempted in her life. "I'm afraid there won't be time for us to visit as we usually do."

Anson

Anson paused, savoring her obvious disappointment. Deborah's life was changing, and it couldn't be avoided. Lady Kringle intended for her daughter to grow up and assume her place in society. Her taking to her bed in feigned illness at such a crucial time proved that point, if Deborah's reading of the situation was correct (and he had no reason to believe it wasn't). Their time for romping and playing had ended. And her disappointment at sending him away sounded a sweet music to his heart.

Besides, he could always create a new place for himself in her new life. It just had to be the one he wanted, rather than one dependent upon *someday* and *perhaps*.

Nor could he bring himself to worry about Deborah, the creative, stubborn, wonderful creature he loved. "Organizing the Christmas Eve ball? You'll do splendidly."

She blinked twice. "What makes you think that?"

"You always do." It was nothing but the truth.

More blinking, and he realized with horror that she fought tears. A rush of fear stabbed through him, dismantling all his emerging plans. "You did say your dear mama—"

She shook her head and brushed the tears away. "She didn't even have the grace to skip breakfast this morning. George, will you be at Lady Gower's garden party tomorrow?"

"Well, it's going to rain, so it will be a garden

party in her parlor." He grimaced. Lady Gower, having survived all her husbands, had nothing better to do than entertain, and she did so pretty much without surcease. "But yes, I'll be there."

"Good. I can't avoid it, so we'll find a handy corner and talk more then." She rose, drawing him with her. "Right now, among a hundred other errands Mama hasn't bothered to perform, I must go and order the new candles for the ball."

Sensing an opportunity, he grinned. "The famous vanilla-scented ones?"

Her eyes narrowed. "I don't like vanilla. This year they'll be mint."

She intended to break with tradition. Good for her! "Well, then, may I have the honor of escorting you to town?"

She froze, a myriad of emotions clouding her face: surprise, concern, doubt, wonder. For a moment she examined him as if she'd never seen him before, while his heart pounded a strange and staccato beat. His nightmare had always been that, when he first demonstrated his intention to court her, she'd turn her back and walk away. A little portion of his soul peered from around a cowardly corner and waited for her first glance aside. The chance of someone so wonderful returning the affection of someone like him... well, it just wasn't likely, was it?

Then her beautiful face cleared with a smile, and it felt as if the sun came out and shone on him alone. And if the change truly did paint such a beautiful picture, why did his heart ache so?

"Of course you may, George, and thank you. I'll want better help sorting out the numbers we'll need than the footman or coachman would offer. And I refuse to drive out to Hampstead for the task, to Mama's preferred chandler, when Mayfair's so much more fun."

He forced a return smile, but disappointment tightened his chest in a painful squeeze. She acted as if nothing had happened, as if their friendship could continue without change. It was a bitter blow, even though he had no idea what response on her part would have made his smile natural and gleeful. What could she have said or done to prevent his sudden despair? He didn't know, and that made it even worse.

If only he could *someday* be more to her than good old George, helpful on errands and fun about town. But with the worries crowding her, now wasn't the most appropriate time, and her gentle refusal to notice his offer proved that.

He would ride in the carriage with her and her maid. He'd keep her company, cheer her as much as possible, carry whatever needed carrying, and escort her wherever she needed to go. And he'd keep his courting to himself for now. She needed room and time to adjust to her new life. Once that life was organized and ready, *perhaps* he'd find a spot within it for himself.

Someday.

Chapter Eleven

Deborah

Wednesday morning, November 24, 1813

The Holly Hall carriage dropped the vegetable cook off at the market, her slate with its chalked list clutched in one hand and her final glance back at them—*alone in a carriage! alas, the young mistress is ruined!*—speculative at best. Deborah sniffed. Straight out of one of Frederick Shaw's Gothic romances, that thought was. What on earth was she thinking? She'd never before cared what society thought, much less the vegetable cook, and this wasn't the first time she'd ridden alone with George. It shouldn't matter.

But for some reason, this time it did.

As soon as the carriage eased forward again, heading toward Mayfair, she yanked down the blind, abandoned her seat, and joined George on his, lowering the second blind in passing. Enough lame chatter about the clouds gathering on the horizon and poor Lady Gower, silly enough to host a garden party in November. They had real matters of importance to discuss. It would be best if the West End didn't observe them huddling over secrets; it would be bad enough when they stepped from the carriage, with all those people around and the *Chatterer*'s note that morning.

She swung sideways on the seat and leaned in toward him—and instantly regretted it. George's face waited bare inches away, beautiful eyes widening, one of those sportsman's shoulders even closer and his left hand sitting casually on the seat between them. If she liked, she could slip her fingers through his, or run her hand up his arm, or... Jolts of heat rippled through her. The temptation was real, in her body and not her imagination, and she clasped her hands in her lap. He wanted their friendship to remain the same. She would honor his wishes, no matter how little she liked it.

And at the moment, she liked it very little indeed.

"Forgive me if I've shocked you, George." She sat back into the seat's corner, putting space between them before she succumbed to the temptation, accidentally or otherwise. "We have a lot to discuss and once we leave the carriage, there won't be much privacy granted us. May we speak frankly?"

He shook his head, as if shaking off water, then grimaced. "Of course. Where shall we start?"

"Why on earth is Mama doing this?" She had intended to start with the love letter and learn his thoughts on that intriguing subject, but her mouth blurted out something else first. Perhaps that was the one closest to her heart?

And perhaps she didn't know herself nearly as well as she thought.

A gentle smile crossed his face. His soft voice matched it. "Deborah, my dear, that's the easy part. She wants you to grow up."

It stung—she *had* grown up, quite nicely, thank you very much—and she sniffed. "What would be the point? I've no real accomplishments, no abilities worth the having—"

She always said something similar when the topic of discussion turned in that ugly direction. But this time, he didn't roll his eyes and tilt his mouth into a rueful smile, as she expected. Instead, he surprised her with a firm shake of his head.

"That's not true. You're clever and resourceful, and you'll manage this ball with half your brain tied behind your back."

Stunned, she could only stare at him while the compliment trickled through her thoughts. "If that were so, then one would expect such a paragon to trail a score of successful entertainments in her wake—"

"You've never tried before."

It was impossible to argue with his flat, factual tone of voice. All she could do was glare at him. He'd taken the conversation in a direction she hadn't intended, and it irked her, no matter what flattering things he said. And flattery his words surely were.

But hadn't she been considering something similar—a husband, children, a household of her own—just the previous evening?

He didn't even return her scowl. "Don't bite my head off. It's only the truth."

Anson

Deborah's scowl didn't waver. Anson hadn't intended to irritate her, but it seemed incredible that she hadn't deduced Lady Kringle's goal herself. After all, if *he* could do so... But she'd been distracted by so much—her dear mama's collapse, real or feigned, the literary salon and now the Christmas Eve ball, that blasted love letter and Cumberland's prank—so perhaps it shouldn't surprise him.

He eased further back along the seat. And *perhaps* his blood would quit boiling with urgency before they left the carriage. Then again, with her sitting so close…

But she leaned forward into the space between them. "If you're so clever, who do you think wrote that love letter?"

He'd intended to ease the conversation in that direction, but fighting the urge to yank her closer—much closer—distracted him, and instead it came out bluntly. "That's easy, too. Cumberland, who else?" Oh, not good. It sounded as if he boasted, and he of all people had no right.

She froze, jaw dropping. "In your handwriting?"

"He's certainly received enough invitations from me over the last two years, since I set up house. I have no doubt of his artistic ability and copying handwriting can't be much harder than copying a painting." Anson paused, drew a breath. The wonder growing in her eyes as she stared at him… no, he needed to concentrate on their subject, not on the beautiful woman sitting so close. But he couldn't force himself to look away, nor forget her. An awareness of her consumed him, like a fire.

Thankfully, the carriage rocked to a stop, shaking him from his Deborah-induced daze. A crunch from the back alerted them that the footman had jumped down, and in a flash she slid back onto her seat. When the carriage door opened, she lounged into the corner as if she'd never moved.

"The chandler's, miss." The liveried footman lowered the step and moved aside.

Anson breathed a sigh of relief, then another when she took the footman's hand to step down, rather than wait for his. But still, the image of her figure, silhouetted against the afternoon's glow… clearly he'd been born to suffer.

In the chandler's emporium, filled with the myriad scents of musk and flowers and hot wax, they pored over the numbers she'd brought and did the math, adding in extras for decorations and a few more for good luck. They stood so close, Anson had no difficulty separating her subtle perfume from the olfactory haze. A sweet torture, that was.

"And make them mint scented, please," she said at last.

The chandler reared back. "Not vanilla?"

Anson bit off a smile. Everyone had heard of that particular tradition of Lady Kringle's, it seemed. Or maybe the man had merely heard of his Hampstead competitor's massive order at this time every year.

Deborah sniffed, then sneezed. "No. Not vanilla."

Outside on the pavement, she paused and examined the little paper she'd brought, covered with notes, scrawls, blotches, and crossed-out words, now scrunched into a careless ball. "Everyone's handwriting varies," she said, "depending upon what you're writing at the moment. For example, my shopping list here looks very different from any letter I'd let leave the house." She glanced up, peered into his eyes, and paused again, this time for such a long moment he wondered if she'd finished her thought after all. But her lips eased apart, slowly widened, so he waited and tried not to stare at that luscious temptation. Finally she said, her voice strangely breathy, "On the love letter, was that your invitation handwriting?"

"Yes, it was." She used *that word* so casually it hurt. Anson cleared his throat. "A formal invitation, at that—not one to an intimate friend."

Her smile flashed and she paused yet again, lengthening her stare. Around them, the bustle of Oxford Street faded away, and he found himself sharing the moment with her, enjoying her company in a way he hadn't for days. Whatever else happened, it seemed their friendship would survive, and that warmed him more deeply than... drat it all... than the way she again stood too close to him, and this time on a very public street.

Then her brows twisted. "Why, though? Why on earth did he do that?"

Anson stepped back with a sigh of relief, suddenly more aware of the bustling shoppers around them than before. Were they all staring? Of course they were, and heat invaded his face. "Well, there I'm not certain." He kept his voice low. It was too much to expect privacy on Oxford Street, but he had no reason to broadcast their business as if cheering a cricket match. "At first I thought he was still angry with me for serving as Rainier's second in that ridiculous duel. But if that were the case, then he'd have no reason to drag you into the fray, would he?"

"Unless he just wants to be outrageous?" She shrugged, but her gaze lingered on him. Was her expression softer than before? "Sometimes one does, you know."

Tempting, to blacken the blackguard's name further. But honesty compelled him. "Cumberland's a rake and a cove, without doubt. But I can't think of a single time when he's been rude to a lady. Can you?"

With a scowl, she turned down the sidewalk and started walking. "No."

Deborah

"It just seems a very odd thing for any man to do, much less a duke," Deborah said.

They sauntered down the sidewalk together, hopefully toward the spice store. She found herself uncertain whether she had turned them in the proper direction or not. Even with the press of errands lined up for them, she didn't care. A few minutes with George, sorting out the questions that plagued her, wasn't too much to ask.

He swung sideways, facing her as they walked, his eyes alight. "Odd, yes, that's it exactly. During the snack break at your literary salon, when I cornered Cumberland—you remember—"

"Oh, do I ever."

"—he behaved rather oddly then, too." But then George's face closed itself off and a tinge of red stained his cheeks. He looked away, started to speak, changed his mind, and started again. "Like your suspicions, it's nothing I can actually explain, more a feeling than anything else. But it's like he's playing with other people's lives because he doesn't like his own."

Her next step refused to come. All Deborah could do was stare at George as the image he'd sketched for her worked itself out in her mind. There were times, widely spaced moments but undeniably there, when Cumberland... *changed*, lost his smugness, his playfulness. He became different, less confident and cynical, more young and lost. The change lasted mere moments, and then his bland smile inevitably returned. Was the face he showed Mayfair merely a façade? Did a deep unhappiness reside beneath his sunny surface veneer?

How had she ever considered George Anson a buffoon? He proved to have far more wisdom than she, and clearly his mental wanderings through their situation had achieved far more success than hers. She'd underestimated him—she, his closest friend. Even if her romantic imaginings never bore fruit, she owed him more respect.

And no matter what, she wanted this man—the one she knew so well and who gave her so much comfort—to hold a permanent place in her life. As her beloved, if the great uncaring universe cooperated. If not, as a friend.

For now, their relaxed relationship could remain. But not forever.

Anson

"Do you think Cumberland's ever been in love?"

She threw the question out so casually. It was impossible to believe any other meaning hid within her plain, simple words. But heat invaded Anson's face, regardless.

"I do," he managed to say, then regretted his choice of words. He *wouldn't*, not with his wood nymph, not if he didn't sort out how to woo her, and unfortunate hints like that wouldn't help his situation. Anson cleared his throat, opened the spice shop's door for her, and tried again. "I think he's been badly disappointed, too."

"In love?" If Deborah had even noticed his gaffe, she ignored it with good grace and better humor. She didn't even throw him a teasing glance. Indeed, she strode past him into the shop and so turned further away from him, denying him any glimpse of her expression. The shop's scents filled his head, so many he couldn't pick out a single one, the same way too many thoughts filled his mind and too many emotions his heart. "In what way?" she asked.

Anson swallowed. Well, Cumberland had implicated himself at the literary salon with his strange comment, and he'd not requested it be kept in confidence. But still, it felt wrong to expose him. "I got the impression he didn't speak up at the right moment."

She froze in midstep, as if trying to decide where in the dim shop the proprietor hid. And Anson's heart froze in his chest to match, for very different reasons. But no... the moment wasn't right.

Was he so certain he'd recognize the moment when it came? What if it never did? Could a moment be forced or created? How?

And had Cumberland asked himself the same questions, in the years since his moment had passed him by?

The only thing of which Anson was certain was the bitter scent of rue when he leaned over its tub. Oh, yes, and of one more thing: he wanted this woman in his life. Somehow, some way, whether as beloved or as friend, he'd find a way to hold her and not let her go.

Chapter Twelve

Deborah

Wednesday, November 24, 1813

"The final, unfortunate question is, what can we do about all this?" Deborah asked.

They'd left the spice shop behind and paused for a break in the traffic to cross Oxford Street. The well-known Holly Hall carriage waited on the pavement's other side, ready to whisk them off unchaperoned to the Robinsons' linen-draper's shop. Considering all the smirks and sideways glances the passers-by awarded them, everyone else foresaw the next actions George and she would take—cross the street, enter the carriage—perfectly clearly. Perhaps they wondered if a few naughty actions might not follow once the door closed on them. The *Chatterer* had never before enjoyed such a wide readership, it seemed.

She shouldn't care. She'd never cared before. But now, for some reason, it all mattered. The fun and playful world she'd created for herself was crashing down around her ears and she could think of no way to stop it.

And so she might as well grow up.

It was funny how she and George discussed every possible subject except the one weighing on her mind, the one she could find no way to broach—their friendship and the changes it needed to survive.

"Yes, that's the problem, isn't it?" George scuffed at the curb and grimaced. "I'd thought of following Rainier's example and calling Cumberland out—"

She shuddered. Everyone knew Cumberland had volunteered with the King's German Legion in the Peninsular War. Everyone knew him to be an experienced soldier, a crack shot, and a strong swordsman. Rainier knew it most clearly of all. "Don't even consider it."

"Good." The relief in Anson's voice was impossible to miss. "I'd much rather not. So if we're not going to be high-minded like Rainier, what can we do?"

She sighed and spoke her first thought aloud. "It's too bad we can't pass a hint on to the *Chatterer*. I mean, the strategy worked so well for him."

The break in traffic came, two phaetons rattling past and drawing away, and she started across the street. It took a few steps before she realized George didn't cross at her side. She paused in the middle of Oxford, turned, and glanced back. His stare at her seemed fixed, and even in the darkening afternoon light as the clouds moved in, she couldn't miss the color growing in his cheeks.

"George?"

With a start, he ran a few steps and joined her, then rolled his lips together and popped his eyebrows. "What if we could? Get a line in the *Chatterer*, I mean?"

It was like a gaslight flaring to life inside her mind. Still standing in the middle of the road, Deborah clasped his wrist, in full view of everyone strolling about Oxford Street, and squeezed. "You write for them, don't you?"

Shock widened his eyes. "How on earth—"

She smiled. "Because the *Chatterer* never speaks an ugly word about anyone, no matter how well deserved."

Honestly, she should have figured it out ages ago. The *Chatterer*, the most bland of all the gossip sheets in town, could only get its fun and harmless information from someone who thought along those same kindly lines. Deborah shook his wrist gently and released him. Another pack of phaetons approached. They'd better clear the roadway.

"Write to them, George. And here's what I want you to say."

Anson

later that afternoon

"They'll be going to press any minute now." Anson settled the spare saddle on the spare carriage horse's back, making sure the blankets were tucked well into the saddle's throat so the tackle wouldn't bind on the beast's spine. Poor Topper hadn't worn a saddle since she'd come to town. The least he could do was keep the unexpected experience from being painful. She already rolled her eyes back at him.

Vicker shifted beside him, staring up at the horse's topside with his eyes widening further by the second. "You know, I could run all the way—"

"—and whoever that sod has following you could do that, too. No, this is the only way, and Topper's the sweetest horse in the stable." With one sustained pull, Anson tightened the girth.

Like a true drama queen, Topper gasped, braced her legs, threw up her head, and widened her eyes, matching Vicker's.

No, actually she surpassed him. Anson sighed. And now Vicker's eyes were doing their best to out-widen hers. It was a race to see who could show the most dismay, his valet or his spare carriage horse. Oh, what a great combination to turn loose on London's streets without a warning. Perhaps he should go himself... no, so far his secret remained just that, with only four people in the know. If he were seen stopping in at the *Chatterer* with paper in hand, everyone in town would soon figure it out and there would go his unsuspecting sources of information. And really, what harm was he doing, sharing some inoffensive gossip with the town? It had been a lark, and unless some actual harm came from it, he intended enjoying it to the very end.

Besides, while he'd never considered himself a literary sort of chap, with his little notes in the *Chatterer* he'd had the honor of going to press four or five times as often as Frederick Shaw. That was a harmless sort of revenge against all those educated-and-looking-down-their-noses-at-him types.

Granted, he didn't like what this particular note said. He didn't like Deborah's plan at all, but it contained a fitting punishment for Cumberland, a horrific jolt for Lady Kringle, and it gave the situation's upper hand back to Deborah for the lady to do with as she pleased. Oh, *she* liked the plan just fine. But not him.

Topper's head wasn't coming down. Anson stroked her shoulder, caressed down her neck, scratched her withers, and slid a sugar cube from his pocket. She resisted his physical blandishments but at the first whiff of something sweet, her nose swiveled down and bumped his hand.

"There, good girl, you just want some dessert with your work, don't you?" He kept his hand closed around the sugar for a few moments, distracting her from her snit as much as possible. Then he opened his fingers and the cube disappeared. Crunching noises, nodding head, relaxing muscles—there, he'd made someone happy, at least.

A quick tug dropped the stirrup on the near side, then Anson gave the rein and a few more sugar cubes to Vicker. While his valet and his horse made friends, with great crunching and eagerness, he slid around behind Topper and tugged down the other stirrup. A hand pushed beneath the girth showed it to be tight enough, and he led the mare from the standing stall to the stable door, which was still closed. Mama Anson hadn't raised any fools and he wasn't going to give that sod out there any warnings. Whoever Cumberland had following Vicker around, he'd eat dust.

Anson eased the big carriage door open and peered out. One of his footmen lounged against the fence post leading to the outer mews, casually watching beside the open gate. The man didn't look at him, but a gentle headshake showed he took the duty seriously. He'd watched and no one lurked within view.

Maybe Cumberland's spy only followed Vicker on occasion. It didn't matter. That chink in their defenses was going to be slammed shut, and the closer to that scoundrel's nose it slammed, the better.

Anson turned back, gave Vicker a leg up into the saddle, and got him settled while slipping Topper one more sugar cube for luck. "Not going to ask you to gallop all the way, but if you should, there might be a sweetener in this for you, too. And remember—"

"I remember," Vicker said. His grin had appeared with the bribe. "Tell the gents at the shop that if anyone else comes by, saying it's from us, well, it ain't."

Not grammatical, but— "Precisely."

Anson patted Topper once more, hauled the big door all the way open, and stood aside. Her temper truly sweetened, the mare scrabbled past across the brick floor and thundered for the road.

Chapter Thirteen

His Grace

Thursday, November 25, 1813

He'd found it hard to sleep, with memories of home running through his mind all night, and Ernst had no idea if he'd succeeded at all. At first light he saddled Sassenach and rode the big dark warhorse around Rotten Row. Not the rousing gallop he'd have preferred, but the old horse, while always game, deserved some courtesy along with the grey hairs lightening his muzzle. A return to St. James's, a rub down and feed for the horse, ablutions for himself, and perhaps he could do some justice to a meal, as well.

The new *Chatterer* waited beside his plate. It had been folded open, meaning Godric or Thomas or Christopher had read it and found something of interest. Well, it could wait a few moments. The mask of His Grace once more firmly in place, he settled at the table and poured the first cup of coffee, lifted it and sipped while glancing at the paper—

—and spewed coffee all over the table.

Deborah

Just her bonnet and gloves remained, and then she'd be ready, which meant it was time to prepare for her grand exit.

Deborah slid the latest *Chatterer*, carefully folded open, from beneath the hatbox, and handed it to her lady's maid. "Susan, dear, would you give this to Ames and ask him to give it to Mama?"

Susan paused before accepting the paper, and Deborah felt a frisson of worry. Maybe teaching her lady's maid to read hadn't been the smartest thing she'd ever done. But no, she wouldn't regret that. She'd seen Susan entranced by Frederick Shaw's Gothic romances too many times for regret now.

"Yes, I know what it contains," she said, more quietly. "Please hand it on to Ames."

"Yes, miss." Without even a sigh, Susan took the paper and headed toward the dressing room door.

Once the maid was out of sight, Deborah settled her bonnet, pinned it in place, grabbed her gloves, and ran downstairs. Her heart thumped, a strange, heavy sort of rhythm, but not from the exercise. Playful, yes, of course she was, but she had never before played such a public and deliberate prank on her mother, not to mention a flaming duke. Even if she was taking on a grown woman's task with the Christmas Eve ball, this sort of thumb-in-the-eye behavior felt rebellious and daring.

At the newel post she paused. Had that been a crash upstairs?

A yell drifted down. "Deborah! Where is that girl?"

Deborah smiled. A crash, yes, quite possibly it had been, as if her mother had started up from a lazy sprawl and thrown something out of her way.

Deborah tugged on one glove. A commotion wearing her mother's voice was exactly what she wanted to hear.

More yells, the voice now panicky. "Stop her! Stop her *now*!"

Second glove, and oh, what a lovely shade of blue they were. They were the perfect match for her gown, and if she didn't leave now, Ames would cut her off at the door. That thundering sound could only be the poor man frantically galloping down the stairs behind her.

"DEBORAAAAAH!"

At the door, the footman seemed undecided between holding it open or closing it in her face. She slipped through before he made up his mind and danced down the steps to the carriage.

It was going to be a glorious day, even if it did look like rain. Points to George, there.

Deborah

The usual crush of carriages crowded before Lady Gower's little front garden, everyone trying to get as close as possible as fat drops of rain splattered the sidewalk. Deborah peered out the side window. Steam rose from the horses' backs, warming the chilly air. And the whispering... she could *feel* it, before ever she left the Holly Hall carriage. The press of quiet voices rolled from the town house, a constant flood of gossip from this, the center of London's never-ending gossip.

She sighed. She *would* pick Lady Gower's party to go on the offensive. Well, she'd just have to suffer through it.

The carriage stopped, the footman dismounted,

and then he opened the door and stuck his head in. "There's no getting closer, miss, and it wouldn't be right to leave the horses standing long enough to try." He grimaced. "But I brought an umbrella. A really big one."

"That's fine, Gowdy. If you'll walk me in?"

It was a big umbrella indeed, and it covered her and her blue gown with inches to spare. Even after the footman had escorted her to the front door, she remained comfortably dry. But the silent flood of curiosity rolling from the house reached overwhelming proportions, and Deborah had to remind herself that it was, after all, her own idea. And with her first step over the threshold, she heard it.

"There she is!"

"She does look lovely in that soft blue. Why, she doesn't seem pale or interesting at all!"

"How on earth do you think she managed the feat?"

And *there*, across the vestibule in the arched doorway leading to the staircase, a pair of icy pale blue eyes met hers. He'd been waiting for her, like a good ducal fiancé should, even one who'd learned of his fate—er, his *engagement* through a gossip sheet. George had sent a note to the *Chatterer*, advising them that "the noble C. has become entangled in Hymen's flower garland at last, alongside Miss D.K. of Hampstead's Road." Of course the *Chatterer* was read over breakfast throughout the West End, so now the information was everywhere, whether it was correct or otherwise. So unless he wanted to throw her off in the middle of Lady Gower's garden-party-in-the-parlor... but as George had said, Cumberland had never been publicly rude to a lady.

Despite her clenching stomach, Deborah's smile burst free and she rushed across the vestibule, stopping so suddenly and so close that her swishing gown curled over his pumps like a sighing wave at the shore.

"Darling, here you are!" She slid her hand up his arm—at least up his claret-colored sleeve, but she couldn't miss the tense muscles underneath—and batted her eyelashes at him. The plan had been for her to flirt with him and convince everyone that the news was true—and then dump him in a week and let everyone make of that whatever they would. Unfortunately she hadn't had much practice at flirting, so her actions more likely came across as awkward or silly, but there, she'd given it a shot.

Cumberland blinked. For a second his expression turned flat, as if she'd utterly surprised him. Then the ice in his eyes melted by a single degree, and while he didn't precisely smile, his tightened lips relaxed and started to curl. "My dear Deborah."

He bowed over her hand, and even through the blue gloves, his breath tickled the sensitive skin there. She shivered, a delicious thrill radiating from the spot he kissed to the rest of her, faster than a charging pack of foxhounds. She and George hadn't been able to guess how Cumberland would respond. Astonishing, it was, that he took the prank so well; an announcement of his entanglement in the *Chatterer*, of all places, must have made his breakfast one to remember. Then again, maybe he was in shock. To her certain knowledge, no young lady had ever turned the tables on him before. A good feeling, that little victory.

Around them, the crowd in the vestibule had fallen silent. She had no need to look. She could feel the stares, the smirks and sideways glances, just as she'd felt the gossip before she had ever stepped from the carriage. If anyone present had smirked and sideways-glanced at her and George on Fleet Street the day before, surely their confused expressions dotted the otherwise uniform crowd.

Cumberland offered his arm and she took it, letting him lead her around the corner, up the stairs, and into the formal drawing room. The elaborate woodwork's gilt scrolling glowed beneath massive sticks of candles, necessary because of the darkening day outside, and the shepherds and nymphs flirting in the murals between panels seemed to tilt and bend in the flickering light. Deborah could swear the glittering eyes of the dragon hovering in one scene winked at her in passing.

And there, by the white marble fireplace with its towering overmantle—George watched them, not even bothering to hide it. And the unhappy emotion souring his expression—

Deborah looked away, the candlelight swinging around her. What could have caused such misery in good-natured George Anson? And why had her heart chosen then to start beating so hard, so heavily?

A weight settled on her hand, where it curled around Cumberland's elbow, and patted twice. "For the sake of my reputation," he said in a dry voice that couldn't be heard a foot away, "our engagement cannot last long."

Oh, that brought a smile to her face. "Your reputation? Are you implying that the possibility of a lasting arrangement between us would ruin you or something?"

"That would depend upon any excesses in your spending." His glance down at her radiated amusement, although his lips barely curled. It all shone from his eyes, and if she weren't mistaken, the glint growing behind the fun showed a blossoming admiration, or at least respect. "You don't shop to excess, do you?"

That delicious shiver down her back repeated itself, stronger this time, and warmth flowed behind it. It was tempting to reach up and tease the dark curls brushing his black leather collar. Was a fiancée permitted such liberties? "Everyone knows I hate spending my pin money. Unless it's on pins, of course."

"Then rumors of my ruination are vastly overrated. No, I've worked very hard for this reputation, and I have no intention of allowing you to alter it, for better or worse."

Oh, how she yearned to ask for the reasons behind his cultivating of a disreputable reputation! But there, discretion seemed the better part of valor. Besides, the heat still spreading through her, centering in parts of her anatomy she didn't normally consider, made playing in his hair a bad move indeed. Already her awareness of his body, so close to hers, threatened to interfere with her bantering, and her breaths tended to hitch in her throat. Something about Cumberland, something inherently and powerfully masculine, affected her thinking at this closer range, rather like her nearness to George the previous day had affected her. It wouldn't do to lose her concentration and make a real fool of herself, more than she already was.

Handsome, oh, yes, Cumberland qualified for the word. The dark hair, straight on top and curling at the ends, against his strong tan and stronger face, could not help but draw the eye. Wide cheekbones, narrow lips, a manner that could only be described as courtly, at least when he wasn't ravishing some poor gentlewoman from across the room with his stare... no, she couldn't believe that rumor about him being a foreign prince, but in every other respect he was a magnificent catch. And for the moment, he was all hers.

What if she didn't release him from her enforced entanglement? Oooh, that thought intensified the heat sliding through her. Mama would, of course, have a conniption fit, finishing off her pretended illness as the lie it surely was.

Deborah shivered and without thinking, she glanced at George. He hadn't moved, and his fixed stare from across the crowded formal parlor, between moving bodies and above swaying heads, reminded her of Cumberland's long-distance ability to ravish. She shivered again and looked away.

Slowly they sauntered around the room, her arm curled around Cumberland's elbow, his free hand atop hers and holding her close. She forced herself to watch the passing murals rather than her handsome escort, and thankfully the painted scenes never quite became bawdy, not like Lady Baldwin's ceiling frescoes; that would have undone her, indeed. But then they reached the corner and without thinking she glanced to the right, the natural direction for them to turn, and there stood George, still watching beside the fireplace. His face seemed carved from the same white marble as the mantle and outer hearth, as if something angered him. But his beautiful brown eyes reflected pain.

Deliberately she again looked away. Surely he'd understand and not hate her for it. Everything she did during this week was a blow aimed at Cumberland and Mama, and George knew that. He had to know it. They had discussed it most fully. Neither of them had to like it. They merely had to ruin Cumberland's week as he'd ruined theirs.

Wait—George was angry? That didn't seem right. But when she permitted herself another peek at his corner, the lines of his face had hardened even more, putting the gleaming marble to shame.

She was looking at George more than her supposed fiancé, and that would fool no one, not even herself. It hurt, but she turned Cumberland to face her, putting his body between her and George's corner. "You know, if you break the engagement, such as it is, I'll out you."

Cumberland's pale eyes widened further. The ice she'd seen there earlier had all melted away, leaving a glint that contained both admiration and rue. "Out me?"

"Your hobby, actually. With how many couples have you played this matchmaking game?"

There—the moment she'd awaited. The smug, amused mask fell away, and for a second the man who stood before her... changed, somehow. The lines of his face remained the same, a strong face, those broad cheekbones and that Grecian nose, and in the flickering candlelight his coloring did not fade. But the smile, the confidence, the easy assurance of superiority all vanished in that second, and the wistfulness, the dismay, that replaced it...

She'd remember that moment and that face for the rest of her life.

But then his jaw hardened. A flame reflected from his eyes, turning them briefly scarlet, and they narrowed as if he reckoned his vengeance on them, George and her, for their presumption. Deborah shivered again, not with delicious sensations but with sudden fear. This duke, this man—this soldier, she'd never seen him before, and she never wanted to meet him again.

As quickly as it came, though, it passed. Cumberland's smile spread, lightening his face. "The lady is always in charge. At least for now."

Her innards refused to stop quaking. Seeking comfort, she glanced around the claret-colored sleeve toward George's corner. But it was empty. He'd left.

Chapter Fourteen

Ernst

Thursday evening, November 25, 1813

"Well, *of course* he's not in a prison cell."

The Prussian courtier had arrived at the perfect hour in the evening for a supper invitation to come naturally from the host and be impossible to refuse for the guest. And so he had stayed for supper, and now they sat before the hearth, decanter between them and fire crackling, in the rear sitting room. It was Ernst's favorite room in the massive house in St. James's Square, and it would be forever defiled with the evening's memory.

He should never have given in to those inner hospitable promptings, but he hadn't even taken a moment to consider. A visitor from the Continent, someone with knowledge of home, how the last battle had gone, the current dispensation of Napoleon's retreating troops—*please, stay for supper* had seemed the right, natural, and necessary thing to say.

That had been two hours ago. Now Ernst clasped his hands in his lap. The alternative was to strangle his guest, answering the insult neatly and illegally, for the news he had brought deserved nothing less. The Prussians had arrested and imprisoned his father.

But seven years ago, it had been the cowardice of some senior Prussian officers, when they'd run for safety from the twin battles of Jena and Auerstädt, that had plunged Saxony into war on Napoleon's side in the first place. For them to imprison his father now, after they'd caused the problem... that affront could only be answered in blood. But if he indulged that desire in London, he'd be arrested himself and join his father in condition if not in location... unless he hid the body really well.

Rage pounded through him, cold and distant, like ocean waves beating at the foot of a cliff. He knew it didn't penetrate through his invisible mask, the one he'd perfected as a child at court and hid behind still to baffle Napoleon's spies. The craven representative of a dishonorable government currently sitting at his hearth could not be permitted to see the reaction his despicable conversation had aroused.

The Prussian courtier, Herr von Dombardt, turned the brandy glass in his hands, as if admiring the alcohol's sparkling amber color against the flames. "*Ach*, don't misunderstand me deliberately, your majesty. Your royal father suffers no hardships and barely an inconvenience. No one treats a king with discourtesy."

He'd emphasized the point all evening, as if to drive home the fact of his father's humiliation. Frederick Augustus, King of Saxony and former Elector of the Holy Roman Empire, had been arrested in mid-October by the Prussians after his troops deserted him during the Battle of Leipzig—or, as the press had begun calling it, the Battle of the Nations.

Ernst had heard—everyone had heard—of the battle, Napoleon's first, astounding defeat, when the dispatches had finally reached England, three weeks ago. But the only news of Saxony had been of her defeat alongside the tyrant who'd forced her and her armies into the battle and the war in the first place. His worries over his family—father, mother, younger brother, beautiful little sister—had never been slight. Now they ate him alive, from the inside out. When a king suffered such an overwhelming defeat... well, Louis XVI hadn't been the first king to have his head handed to him. Literally.

"For a king, you know, imprisonment can barely deserve the term." Herr von Dombardt heaved a heavy, theatrical sigh, the ends of his curled grey mustaches curling further, as if he smiled beneath their covering. "He may be called a prisoner, but he remains a king always."

The words von Dombardt didn't say hung in the air between them: *even if that king was awarded his crown by an illegitimate emperor only a handful of years ago.* Of course the major Continental nations, Austria and Prussia, would respect such a king. *Of course* they would, and a frisson of fear shivered through Ernst's rage.

Frederick, called *the Just* by his people, did not deserve such a fate.

"A king always," von Dombardt repeated, drawing out the final word with a hiss: *alwaysssss.* "No one would offer him insult. No one would dare! He will be treated as he deserves until this ungodly mess is straightened out."

Ernst's little courtier's smile, the smile of His Grace, widened enough to demonstrate he'd heard the voice speaking if not the words themselves. Inside, he boiled. Not a word of his family, whether they'd accompanied Father to Berlin, where the Prussians held him, or if they remained in Dresden. Not a word of whether they'd even survived the war, much less the Prussian occupation of Saxony. Von Dombardt's intended message, the unspoken one, wasn't a message of comfort, but of acid and malice. Prussia hungered for territory. They'd be perfectly happy to declare Frederick no longer a king, to annex Saxony for their own. And everyone knew what happened to kings who lost their thrones.

And of course, not a breath about Ursula. In all the heady events of the war, who had time or concern for the younger daughters of minor nobles? They were the focus only of lovelorn suitors who lived hundreds of miles away in comfort and elegance while his homeland fell apart without him.

His first yearning, to strangle von Dombardt where he sat, then run home and put everything right with whatever means presented themselves, had to be fought. He didn't even know the details of the circumstances into which he'd be running. Information—he had to know more before making plans.

But if he surrendered and asked von Dombardt the questions which burned within him, it would be a surrender indeed, as disgraceful and defeated as Father's on the battlefield at Leipzig. At Jena in 1806, Ernst had tried to hold the line after the Prussian officers he'd been so proud to call his allies had turned tail and galloped for home. He'd been sixteen at the time. He would follow his own example now, not theirs. He would hold the line rather than run for home.

He would save Saxony, somehow. But he'd do it without the Prussians, and to spite them. All of them—Napoleon, his spies, his deserters covering the territory between Saxony and France, the Prussian army now in occupation there—all of them could go to the devil. He'd find the information he needed elsewhere and then he would head for home.

After he found a way to break his unwanted engagement to the Honorable Miss Deborah Kringle, of course.

Ernst let his smile die—he didn't want to look too welcoming—and lifted the decanter from the little table beside his chair. "More brandy?" If the man were drunk, perhaps his tongue would loosen.

Deborah

The argument with Mama, after she'd left the garden-party-in-the-parlor and returned home to Holly Hall, still burned in Deborah's ears.

"You will call off this—this outrageous engagement immediately!" Lady Kringle had risen from her sickbed and wrapped an embroidered silk robe around herself for the battle. She hadn't seemed pale before, when she'd at least pretended to be ill. Now her color flushed up her neck to her forehead. She prowled beside the window like a caged panther, her steps long and angry, then she whirled at the wardrobe and paced back. The flaps of her robe flared around her legs. "I tell you, Deborah, I will not have it."

Deborah had remained unmoved. "You cannot stop me."

At the flat words, calmly stated (and oh, did she feel sinful pride at that self-control), Lady Kringle froze and stared. Her nostrils quivered, as if the big cat scented prey. "You see if I can't."

But the display of maternal temper had fallen short of cracking Deborah's determination. Mama had lost her previously unquestioned claim to obedience when she'd resorted to a cheap and cruel trick to teach her daughter a lesson. Respect, yes, that remained, for Mama remained an amazing and capable woman. But her theatrical collapse at the newel post had changed everything between them.

Deborah didn't even straighten. She'd drawn her battle lines and she knew in her soul they would not break. "All I must do is wait a few years until I'm one-and-twenty. Then I can marry whomever I like."

The first, and worst, of the fury drained from Mama like milk from an overturned bottle, leaving her white and still frozen in place. She rolled her lips together and swallowed, her throat bobbing with jerky motions. "Do you truly believe Cumberland will wait so long?"

"It's my choice." And it was. A man of honor could not call off an engagement to a lady without cause. If she preferred, she could keep Cumberland dangling for years. Granted, clever as he was, he could manufacture cause without effort, and the thought of what such *cause* would do to the shattered remnants of her reputation moved her, shifting her in place, as all Mama's words hadn't. "You wanted me to grow up, yes? Well, you've succeeded. You should be pleased."

At those words, the last of the color had drained from Lady Kringle's face. Deborah had waited a few seconds, ensuring her mother's lesson had been fully learned, then she'd left, closing the door with quiet care behind her.

She'd thought to go to her rooms and pout, but in the corridor she'd felt no need. Instead she'd gone to the morning room, lit a stick of candles against the darkening sky, and settled at Mama's desk. Impossible to finalize the ball's guest list and seating arrangements so far in advance, but getting her first thoughts down on scraps of paper would prevent those thoughts from being blown out of her mind by the emotional storm whirling inside her.

And yet she'd barely touched quill to paper. During the row, she'd stood easily against Mama's rage. But once she'd sat at Mama's desk, her knees had started shaking and didn't want to quit. Her mother's actions had upended their relationship. Her own threatened to destroy it.

Was that what she wanted? But no, the more accurate question was, was that what it would take for her to wriggle from beneath the wing of Lady Kringle, society leader and ruler of her family's lives? Deborah hadn't considered it before, but her older sister had married quickly and now rarely called. Had a similar wreck occurred between Sophia and Mama, kept quiet from the rest of the Kringle clan?

Especially from her? Mama wouldn't have wanted to give her ideas, after all.

Deborah rubbed her eyes. She had started adding the names of those newly moved to town to Mama's permanent guest list, and crossing off the names of those no longer suitable or who'd passed on. She hadn't gotten far. Outside, night had fallen. Gowdy, the footman, had closed the windows and drapes an hour ago, then padded away on his silent, discreet feet. A well-favored man, that, and an excellent servant. Surely Ames had noticed him and had it in mind to train him in higher duties than closing windows and escorting a flippant, unrepentant daughter around town.

Strange, but last week she'd have watched Gowdy from the corner of her eyes while he'd worked. After realizing her love for George, and after the intoxicating rush of Cumberland's nearness, she'd barely noticed Gowdy, even when he'd stood mere feet from her. Well, clearly she would not need to worry about ruining her reputation over a footman, then.

Behind her, a throat cleared. It could only be

Ames, meaning a late caller had arrived, and that could only be Cumberland, there to work out their relationship. Deborah hung her head over the household management book and sighed. Another argument... could she handle another? Or more likely, could she fend off that delicious temptation? The man should come with warnings displayed.

"Mister George Anson."

That was not who she'd expected, and a warm flush of delight swept through her, closely followed by a tight sort of quivering shiver, the same sort Cumberland had aroused. Wondering, Deborah twisted in Mama's chair.

Ames had already left, even more silent in his movements than Gowdy. George hovered alone not far inside the door, his hat and cloak still in his hands. With the garden party over, he'd regained his usual high color, although she still didn't know (and had forgotten to wonder) why he'd been so pale then. The sadness in his eyes lingered, as if he'd watched someone kick a puppy. Her guts twisted within her.

"George—" Something was very wrong with her best friend, and she'd been so engrossed with her prank that she had not investigated. Guilt swamped her and she started to stand.

But he raised a hand, stopping her. "No. Of your kindness, please just listen."

It was impossible to refuse him anything, so she settled back into Mama's chair and waited. Her heart beat a confusing rhythm, hard slow thumps against her ribs, trying to force its way from her breast. If she could yank it out and hand it to him, she would.

Maybe that would get his attention.

He'd set the scene for whatever he wanted to say—something important enough to ride out along the Hampstead Road at night—but he seemed uncertain how to begin. George stared at her, his sweet, strong face motionless, for so long that her guilt and concern faded in the distance of her mind. How would it feel to wrap her arms around him, hold him close, and feel their hearts beat in unison?

Her pulse quickened at the thought.

Finally his mouth moved, his lips rolled together, and he shook himself, as if shaking off his own deep thoughts. "I know that what you're doing is what we planned."

His words surprised her. She'd expected him to say… well, perhaps that something had happened to one of his parents, or his best shooting dog, or Plato, his grey hunter. Something that could account for the sadness in his eyes. The plan against Cumberland and Mama, the one they'd worked out while strolling along Fleet Street running her errands—that seemed an unusual reason for such misery and effort on his part.

George hauled in a slow, deep breath. "But I can't be a part of it any longer. If you want to continue the pretended engagement for the week we planned, I understand. I just won't be there to watch it."

And he turned around and walked away.

For a long moment, she couldn't move. Her body utterly refused to respond and she sat sideways in Mama's chair, staring at the empty place he'd left. His words echoed in her thoughts: *I can't… I won't be there…*

He disapproved of her behavior, then. His wiser head—for he had demonstrated his wisdom, far beyond her original image of him as a lovable buffoon—his wiser head had seen the unkindness behind her plan and it refused to permit him to continue. Even though both Cumberland and Mama deserved every ounce of the mortification being heaped upon their heads like glowing coals—

But that wouldn't matter to George. In his straightforward soul, unkindness was just that and nothing more, and always to be avoided. Second thoughts consumed him, leaving her to play out her vengeful prank alone.

No. No, that wasn't what he'd said. His expression hadn't been disapproving, and there hadn't been a hint of sour vinegar in his expression. He'd been sad, or maybe hurt. He'd said he wouldn't be there...

...to watch it happening. He'd said he couldn't watch it, couldn't be an active part of it any longer. He had said it as if the actual act of observing her arm in arm with Cumberland gave him pain, not any considerations of the rightness or otherwise of her behavior.

He'd said he couldn't watch her flirt with Cumberland. And the only reason for such a declaration would be...

Deborah shot from Mama's chair and raced across the morning room, expertly wending her way between the furniture. Down the corridor she ran, her heart thumping harder and faster than ever, across the landing, paneling and portraits blurring past, to the front parlor, and she threw aside the drapes, yanked up the window, and pushed out the shutters. Cold air assaulted her. She ignored it and leaned on the sill, as far out as she dared with the paved carriageway below.

There, at the far end of the park, a flash of lantern light, grey haunches flexing and extending, a dark form astride and another afoot alongside, distant hoofbeats—George on Plato trotting away, with a running footman lighting the path to the Hampstead Road. Only a moment did she see them, then Plato rounded the corner and disappeared into the night.

Deborah

The row with Mama hadn't disheartened her. The glimpse of George and Plato's backs left her exhausted. Really, she had no reason to despair; it wasn't as if George didn't live in Mayfair and she couldn't send him a note hinting for his presence. She'd do that, first thing in the morning, and call off the silly plan if it hurt him so much.

Anything. She would do anything for George, if only he'd continue being a part of her life.

Deborah closed the shutters and window, her hands lingering on the drapes' stiff fabric. Yes, she would do anything. And that included making the man she loved see sense—convincing him to love her in return, rather than keeping their friendship unchanged. Mama had been right about that. It was time for her to grow up and become a woman.

A wife.

With the room closed, only a glow of light spilled into the parlor from the stairwell landing, where a lantern burned all night. The brocade she gripped, normally a flamboyant splash of red, white, and yellow, seemed colorless, shades of grey in the dark. It seemed a good symbol for her life should George absent himself from her presence, even for the threatened week.

George Anson. Lovable buffoon, source of some of the craziest notions in Mayfair, sportsman extraordinaire but no one's idea of a scholar—she couldn't possibly imagine herself happy with George, could she?

Happy with the only man in London willing to romp in public with a girl and not get the wrong idea? Happy with the most good-natured, unassuming sport, one more willing to laugh at himself than at anyone else? With a man who only had unkind words to say about those whose behavior left them open to the censure, such as Culver, and even then not for long?

The spurious argument with Cumberland, back at Lady Gower's rout, was the closest to furious George had ever been, at least in her presence. And she'd seen fashionable cretins laugh in his face. He'd shrugged off their ridicule and sometimes he'd laughed with them. Even during the argument with Cumberland, George had been stiff but proper, never letting his behavior go as others might. As Rainier had done, and surely he carried a scar to remind him.

George was jealous. Not hurt, not sad, but jealous. Maybe he didn't want their friendship to continue as before, not after seeing her with Cumberland. But even if he did, Deborah had no doubts that she could convince him otherwise.

She let the brocade slip from her fingers.

Could she be happy with such a man? How could she not?

Chapter Fifteen

Friday, November 26, 1813

Vicker held up the sober black Melton, with its fashionable lines and subtle stitching. Anson frowned at it. Of course he wanted to dress his best, black was never wrong, quiet elegance was tops, and all that. But he intended to propose that day to the lady who'd worn a scarlet gown to her parents' Christmas Eve ball last year. Somehow he didn't think she'd be impressed with a sober black Melton.

Come to think of it, that Melton symbolized his life rather well. He had not been willing to stand out, sartorially speaking, and so he'd worn it and others like it. He'd kept his behavior within bounds, too, until Deborah had befriended him and drawn him into her playful games. Even then, she had led the way and braved society's wrath. He had merely followed her lead. But if he intended to clear her five-barred gate, he'd have to take some chances.

Doubtless Deborah's plan had its merits, because it was her plan. Clever woman that she was, she would never come up with a stinker. But watching her with Cumberland, arm in arm down the formal parlor's long gallery, standing as a couple in

"

the corner, too close together for any two not lovers—it had wrenched his guts out.

And his actions last night, riding out and stammering some half-witted excuse for abandoning her in the midst of that plan, had been nothing short of silly, and if he hadn't suffered through watching them all day, he would not have so embarrassed himself. No, he owed Deborah an explanation, an apology—and a proposal. Considering the way his heart hammered in his chest, judging by the nerves dancing along his skin, he knew her plan had gone quite far enough, and though she hadn't actually snared Cumberland, she'd well and truly caught *him.*

There was only one thing left to do, even if she did turn her back on him and walk away. Because no matter what she did, he would never admit defeat. He would return and court her again and again, until he wore her down or she married someone else.

"No," he finally said, his heart in his teeth, "not that one. In the back of the wardrobe—bring out the tailor's mistake."

With his eyes bulging out, Vicker looked like an astonished rabbit. He put away the Melton, dug into the wardrobe's innards for a bit, and drew out a wrapped package. With the string untied, the brown cloth fell away.

The dark violet tailcoat wasn't loud, or flashy, or in poor taste. Not at all; it had the same subtle tailoring and cut as the black Melton. But it was *violet,* the shade of a ripe plum, and while, yes, he'd seen others wear the same hue or even a few shades brighter, George had never dared put it on himself, even though the bespoke tailor had sent one 'round. After staring at it in horror, he and Vicker had consigned it to the back of the wardrobe and ignored it.

"Yes," Anson said, and swallowed. "Let's try it."

He held his arms back and Vicker slid the tail-coat up and over his shoulders, settling it into place with a practiced tug. Pewter buttons and a grey leather collar provided a bit of inconspicuous trim—he'd never liked flash, except maybe gold buttons for a formal event—and the color, well, it didn't precisely offend the eye. Once he'd done up the buttons, its contrast with the carefully knotted white cravat and grey breeches seemed... pleasing. It seemed modern, and just a touch daring.

His chest swelled.

"Huh." Vicker scratched his head. "Fancy that."

"I know," Anson admitted. "Who'd've thought it?"

They stared at the mirror's not inelegant reflection together. Finally Vicker shrugged. "Looks good."

"Then that's settled." Anson rummaged through the wardrobe's drawer and found his grey gloves. "I'll need the grey redingote. Then run down and make sure Plato's ready. Remind Swanson to black his hooves well today, all right?"

Deborah

She hadn't gotten much more work done, even after an extra cup of tea and stern words muttered to herself.

Deborah leaned back in Mama's chair and pushed Mama's household management book away. The quill she set in its holder, so as not to drip ink—very well, any *more* ink on Mama's blotter. The standing invitation list had grown by a few names and shrunk by a few more. She'd forgotten someone, and the knowledge banged away in the back of her mind without producing an actual name or face.

Was she thinking of the new maid of honor at the Duchess of Brittany's court-in-exile, the one Lissie and Violetta had exclaimed over? If so, the thought qualified as truly silly. Narcisse d'Oettlinger, Duchess of Brittany, kept her maids close to her vest. The odds of one of them, especially the newest of them, being let loose to attend a ball were slim to none.

With a sigh, Deborah finished off the tea and shoved the cup and saucer aside, too. She would remember the name or face later, hopefully.

Her silly plan had worked. It had paid back both Cumberland and Mama, and she would never forget the shrill, panicky edge to Mama's voice as she'd yelled down the stairs yesterday morning, nor the ice and sudden implacable steel in Cumberland's face as his younger self faded away. It had been the single most unkind thing she'd ever done, even worse than hiding her older sister's journal and then forgetting where she'd put it. At least she hadn't damaged the journal and after turning the school-room inside out, the housekeeper had found it.

But her current prank had damaged her rela-tionship with Mama. Cumberland of course would accept an apology from a lady, and if he withdrew from her socially, well, that might be for the best. The man was temptation in silken breeches. If she had been of any mind to force a marriage, as Be-atrice had said to Don Pedro in *Much Ado About Nothing*, she would need another husband for work-ing days, because Cumberland was too expensive for casual usage. No, she had no worries on his behalf, and surely Mama would forgive her after the heart-felt apology she intended to deliver.

The worry... the *real* worry, the one that ate at her soul, was George, and herself. She had not realized before how casually cruel she could be, how little she considered consequences to others prior to speaking or acting. But if her reading of his emotions the previous evening held any accuracy, then she had made him jealous, and that meant she had not only injured the man she loved, she'd potentially injured any feelings he had for her as well. And if that were true, the damage done was to herself and her own prospects.

Deborah sighed and slouched back in the desk chair. It was all so complicated, such a horrific mess, and she felt it would take ages before she forgave herself. And the next time she saw George, she owed that excellent man another apology for ever thinking him a buffoon. Surely the thought had been reflected in her previous behavior toward him, and the heat flushing in her face proved that thought to be true.

Yes, an apology, an explanation, and an admission that her plan had gone on for quite long enough. If it, and she, could cause such misery in one day, then no matter how well it worked, it was time to end it.

A note. She'd send him one of her little notes, reminding him of tea time, and...

A delicate throat cleared behind her. Her heart pounding, Deborah pushed herself upright.

Behind her, Ames said, "Mister George Anson."

He didn't hate her. Relief poured through her like a wave pouring into a shoreline cave. He'd come to call without waiting for an invitation and so he didn't hate her, and the thought shot her to her feet. She turned. George stood in the doorway, resplendent in one of those new purple coats, his cravat perfect as always. But his lips pinched together and the sadness in his eyes had deepened overnight.

Without stopping to think, Deborah reached for

him as she strode across the morning room. Some hazy thought in her head intended only to welcome him—George had come to call, and that was good, it was right—but the jumble of confusion it joined mixed *welcome* with *love* with *guilt* with *apology* with *worry*, and as she approached her ungloved hands rose higher.

His first sadness lost out to a flash of undisguised happiness, then astonishment and glee, his smile growing and his eyes widening, too, and perhaps he thought about it as little as she did, for his hands reached for hers in return, then they clasped, fingers intertwining, skin to bare skin. It felt so natural, so utterly right and proper, nothing strange or different or complicated about it.

She tugged him down with their clasp as she would Papa, and kissed George on the cheek beside his beautiful lips. His arms wrapped around her, so perfectly, a perfect fit, the soft material of his tailcoat against her cheek, beneath her hands, and there, the strong, steady thumping of his heart.

Deborah leaned against him, her eyes drifting closed, and sighed with bliss. "I'm so glad you're here."

He chuckled, his chest bouncing beneath her cheek. "Got that impression."

Put like that, she couldn't ignore the humor in their situation. George always could make her laugh. She started giggling with him, then opened her eyes and laughed—

—and Ames still stood in the doorway, pale as a ghost. He'd faded into the woodwork so thoroughly, she hadn't even noticed him. Before she could forbid it, he turned and vanished.

Oh, dear, and just when things were progressing so swimmingly. Deborah leaned back far enough to meet George's beautiful eyes. They were still dancing with delight, an undertone of disbelief as he freed one hand and stroked her hair. She had to pause at the gentle rush of love his touch aroused. Now that she'd felt it, she had to wonder how she'd ever lived without his touch.

"We can expect Mama and Papa at any moment, so we've not much time." Strange, how breathy her voice sounded.

His lips rolled together, but his hands resettled around her waist as if they belonged there. "Then I need to say what I came to say."

Such happiness in his face, even with the quick little grimace. He glowed with it, as if a candle of joy had been lit within him. She should have made too-bold overtures toward him ages ago, and if any young lady ever asked her for advice about catching the man she loved...

Without thinking, and without waiting to let him speak first as a good hostess should, she said, "I love you, George."

He chuckled again, one heave of his chest, then his grin broadened. "I've loved you since I saw you in that scarlet gown at last year's Christmas Eve ball. Might have been even earlier, but that's when it hit me, and a ton of bricks barely compares to how hard. Didn't know how to say it, of course. I never do." He tugged her closer, his gaze dancing across her face, as if he wanted to take all of her in but couldn't. "So if I've made a pest of myself—"

If any young lady ever asked her...

"Never, dear." She laid a hand against his cheek, so strangely soft yet rough and whiskery at the same time. She would never get tired of stroking his cheek, nor of their arms around each other, nor of the contented love welling in her chest. "And I'm so very glad you recognized that emotion for what it was, long before I even considered it. That's wisdom, you know."

Another muffled laugh. "Think I've got you fooled."

"I think you've got yourself fooled. Who sorted out Cumberland's motives, after all, and Mama's? It wasn't me. Wisdom isn't education, nor parsing Greek, nor even writing sonnets," and with luck, she'd someday live down that ill-advised literary salon. "Wisdom comes from a good heart, and it's innate, not studied nor learned."

If any young lady...

Downstairs, the bell rang, the soft clear notes trilling through the house. She frowned.

"Yes, there's another interruption coming," George said. His beautiful gaze never left her. He turned his face inside the cup of her palm and kissed it, a longing, lingering touch of his lips against her skin, and the shiver that worked its way up her spine shook away more of her concerns. Finally he turned back and faced her, the short edges of whiskers tickling her palm in passing. "I came to say I love you and ask if you'll marry me." His brow creased. "Should I get down on one knee for that?"

Dear George always could make her laugh. "No."

The crease deepened and alarm froze his face. "No?"

"No, you needn't get down on one knee. Yes, I will marry you." And now her giggling wouldn't stop.

Not until his arms tightened around her, at least. She snuggled against him and let the sensations, his emotions, her emotions, their touching skin, sweep her thoughts away. But one vague thought wouldn't be dislodged.

If any young lady...

"Oh, good."

That was not George's voice. Not Ames', nor Papa's. But masculine, and suddenly it was all too familiar. Deborah's eyes flew open.

Cumberland peered past Ames, his expression a study in mischief and relief. A half-smirk lifted one corner of his lips. "I came to discuss the terms of my surrender." He bowed. "Nice to know that shan't be necessary."

From the safety of her beloved's tightening, possessive arms, she laughed in Cumberland's face. The stray thought finally completed itself in her mind. If any young lady ever asked her for romantic advice, she would send the girl to Cumberland. Who could help more?

"Deborah?" Mama's voice called from the house's depths. Soft footsteps hurried along the corridor, and then she burst into the room, past Cumberland, past Ames standing like an invisible sentry, stopping so suddenly that her ribbons twitched. For a moment she stood motionless, staring, and Deborah's heart pounded beneath that maternal stare.

Then Mama sighed and smiled. "Deborah, dear, my dear George, I'm so happy for you." Mama stepped closer, resting a hand on each of their shoulders. If she had any qualms about having George Anson—*George Anson*—for a son-in-law, not a bit of it showed. No, indeed, Mama seemed truly satisfied, bone-deep delighted, as if her dearest wish stood before her, and the last of Deborah's resentment melted.

Deborah slid one hand free from around George's waist, kissed her fingers, then touched them to Mama's cheek. Moving her lips only, she mouthed *I'm sorry.*

Mama's face crumpled. Her eyes gleamed, suddenly too wet. She mouthed *I'm sorry, too.*

But that would never do. Kringle women simply didn't disgrace themselves by weeping in public, and a part of her remained all too aware of Cumberland's silent, surely watching presence. Deborah ruffled Mama's cheek, slid her fingers into that greying coif, and tugged, and then grinned like a monkey when Mama's eyes widened with outraged disbelief.

But before that outrage could find an outlet, Papa strolled into the room, comfortable in a ratty dressing gown and his slippers scuffing across the carpet. Deborah almost squirmed. In front of Mama and Cumberland, the two who had deserved her prank, well, they also deserved to see her snuggling up to George. But Papa...

Oh, dear.

But Papa laughed. "Good on you, George," he said. He glanced aside at Mama, his cheerful smile morphing into an evil little grin. "And good on you, my dear. Your clever little plan worked."

Deborah blinked. She'd never seen that particular smile on her father's face. Then she considered his words. *Wait. Wait one minute.* Her parents had discussed Mama's plan between them? She glared at Mama. "You mean that devious plan to make me organize the Christmas Eve ball?"

But Papa waved a careless hand. "No, not that. That's only a sideline. She was—"

Cumberland interrupted, clearing his throat and crossing his arms. "My dear Lady Kringle, were you perhaps playing *my* game?"

Mama had the grace to redden. "I fail to see how matchmaking is your personal property, your grace. And you were never supposed to play games with my daughter, you know."

"But it was such a perfect situation—"

Papa waved both hands, as if shooing them away. "And don't blame me for any of it, by the way. I'm not an argumentative man, but I promise all of you, I disagreed with her plan and washed my hands of it."

"Leaving me to manage it all on my own." Mama finally disentangled her hair from Deborah's tightening fingers.

The entire situation seemed too ridiculous to be anywhere close to true. Bewildered, Deborah found herself staring at George. He stared back, and with a pang, she realized he had never looked away from her face. His beautiful brown eyes were misty, and her heart double-thumped, took its rhythm from the beat of his heart, beside hers, and she found she no longer cared who else occupied the room with them. It was a moment of magic, straight out of a fairy circle, and she wondered if she and George could dance among the mushrooms with the fair folk.

Then George chuckled—perfect timing, he had—and Deborah began to giggle again through her own threatening tears, and finally Mama joined in, tugging on Deborah's curls in return. If Mama's laughter seemed more relieved than anything else, well, Deborah had to admit the poor woman had had a rough twenty-four hours. For a while there, she'd thought her daughter was engaged to...

Mama's eyes cut sideways. At Cumberland.

Indeed yes, he'd been staring, and remained shameless at being caught. He popped his eyebrows, up and down in a quick, mischievous motion. "I'm leaving."

But Mama hurried over and took his arm, drawing him to her side and summoning Papa to her other with a gesture. "Not like that, you're not. Come, you and I must have some tea together, and a nice long chat."

And there—Cumberland's smugness faded away, taking his worldly wise cynicism with it, leaving the younger man, the hurt and wary one, standing in his place. The younger man stared at Mama, three seconds, four, Mama's shoulders tensing and chin drawing back, and then that man was gone and Cumberland's winning smile flashed across his face.

"A lovely suggestion, Lady Kringle." His brows popped again. "I'm all yours."

She smacked his arm and led him away, but paused in the doorway. "Oh, and Deborah—"

"Yes, Mama, I will finish organizing the ball for you. As my condition, the invitations must have my name on them, not yours. And no, you may not lounge in bed while I do so."

"Agreed." And Mama led Cumberland and Papa away.

Deborah turned back to George. A puzzled crease tangled his forehead, and she had no doubt a similar one graced hers. "You saw?"

He nodded and started to speak, but she laid a finger across his beautiful lips. They were rough and soft at the same time, and a pleasing flush tightened her innards. It was something she needed to examine, that sensation. "Later we'll discuss it. I want your thoughts on that second man living inside Cumberland's skin. But this moment is ours and I'm greedy. I won't share it."

The love in his eyes drew that sensation tighter. An experiment—after all she'd been through, she deserved an experiment. Deborah tugged on George's shoulder. He understood instantly, and she drew his lips down to hers.

From the corridor, a diminishing voice trailed back. "Ames, don't wander from that door!"

Chapter Sixteen

Friday afternoon, November 26, 1813

Another game complete. Another lovely lady's life arranged to her satisfaction and delight, the forces arrayed against her dismayed and routed—

—and he needed to cease thinking in such terms, entertaining though they might be.

Ernst paused in Holly Hall's lavish vestibule, trying to gather his thoughts from the four winds to which Lady Kringle had strewn them. Devilishly clever woman, that. She'd opened their nice long chat with general exclamations over her new son, her happiness at the joining of the Kringle and Anson clans, and she'd put him off guard with her delightful inanities. Then without warning, she'd asked him if he looked forward to going home.

Against such sudden pain, even his court-refined shield hadn't held. Surely the mask of His Grace had crumpled—it seemed to be doing that often lately—permitting her a glimpse of Ernst, hiding beneath it. A compassionate hand on his forearm, a soft, soulful gaze from her motherly eyes, and her spell had been complete. Granted, he had no secrets from Lord and Lady Kringle. They had been among

his first acquaintances in London—in all of England—and he had adored them as a second family
from that first meeting. And their advice, to wait in
London until the situation on the Continent settled
and he knew what he faced—

Well, it was done, and he had let their advice
sway him. And days ago he'd decided that His
Grace, his long-held defense and disguise, needed to
die. With the game over and no more permitted, he
had no excuse for clinging to such a cover. It was
time to remember the man he used to be before he
had drawn on that mask.

Ernst straightened his shoulders, nodded to the
footman, and stepped out the opening door onto
Holly Hall's famous statue-decorated landing.

He froze, heart thudding with a premonition of
dread.

The Duchess of Brittany's carriage waited at the
turn of the drive, that massive enclosed coach with
its six matched grey mares. The crest of plain ermine gleamed gilt and white on the elegant dark
door. The liveried coachman had settled the horses
well—no stamping nor head-tossing among them,
and no footman stood at the lead pair's heads—and
the coachman sat atop the box with the reins between his knees, ready to move them out at a word.

To one side, a groom held Sassenach. His old
warhorse twisted against the rein, his nose pointing
toward the mares.

Ernst stood nonplussed, uncertain if he should
approach or run. The sight of the carriage was so
unexpected that his heart pounded harder, a disquieting sensation that shook him to his soul. His
Grace would—

He shook himself. His Grace was no more.

Something moved in the shadow by the carriage
wheel, and he peered hard, trying to see more than

the gloom permitted. Black it was—black in the shadows, only visible when it moved, a dark cloak, a hood, a swirling hem—

A small figure stepped into the light, slipping the hood from brilliant gold hair, so brilliant it seemed a stray beam of sunlight escaped the autumn clouds and bathed her hair in its warmth. Small, yes, and slender, straight as a sword—

The shock cut through him as if he'd been stabbed in the heart. Ursula. It *was* her, she *was* in London, he *had* seen her, not her ghost, in the foggy nights before All Hallow's Eve. But when he had looked for her in the swirling mist, she'd hidden in its cover, a dark form on a dark night, motionless and not drawing the eye.

She hadn't run to him, not then—and not now. She waited in full view by the carriage, staring at him across the paving, her chin raised. The soft breeze whispered through her tumbled curls, loose around her shoulders and tangled with the hood's folds. Even at the distance, she seemed pale, her Cupid's bow lips darker in the contrast.

Something wasn't right, even though she stood before him, and before he could think it through his feet started without his consent, striding for the stairs, starting down. Once he stood close enough to touch her, whatever troubled her, then he could make it right. He could hold her, comfort her, and his blood fired. Once he stroked her incredible skin, soft and smooth, nothing would dismay her, or him.

But with his first step down the stairs, she whirled. The hem of the heavy cloak swirled about her, the same graceful curlicue that had cut through the mist off the Thames in October, at the time reminding him of her. His heart had known her then by her very movement, but his head hadn't understood.

A second cloaked figure, taller, bulkier, just as disguised by the shadows, emerged from the gloom and opened the carriage door for her. With one hand, the footman—no, the soldier, that military bearing could mean nothing else—the soldier assisted Ursula into the coach.

As she gathered her skirts and stepped in, the officer glanced across his shoulder toward the staircase, hesitating as if uncertain. Ernst froze on the steps, halfway down, meeting the officer's gaze across the distance. A square face, roughened by the wind and weather, sandy hair clipped short, and though they couldn't be seen at the distance, Ernst knew the grey-blue eyes were steady and sober. It was the messenger who had brought her last token to him, back in March.

Had he also accompanied Ursula to London, away from the fighting? Had she been in England that long, and he not knowing?

Then she vanished inside the coach. The officer folded the stairs and closed the door, acting as her footman, and the driver snapped the reins. The six grey mares heaved forward, six off forelegs lifting and striding out together. Sassenach whinnied after them, tugging against the groom. In passing, the officer grabbed the rear seat and hopped aboard with perfect timing. The crest on the door flashed once in the pale light, embedding itself in Ernst's mind.

Well, at least he knew where to find her.

The reins snapped again and the mares swung into a good round trot. The carriage accelerated, the suspension keeping the coach body steady as the wheels rolled over the smooth pavement. Sassenach neighed again. A swing wide, the driver experienced and sure, and then the turn swallowed them, the clopping and rattling disappearing into the distance.

She'd left him.

It was an obvious message, her rejection, angry and abrupt, and Ernst couldn't ignore the equal anger and pain she'd left in her wake. Cold still lined his thoughts, the shock still uppermost, but the first edge of the anger's heat began to defrost him as he stood on the steps of Holly Hall staring after the duchess's coach.

Why had she left without a touch, without even speaking? For seven years he'd waited for her, longed for her, remembered and imagined and remembered again to stave off homesickness.

But no, the more important question was, why hadn't she run to him months ago, when she'd first arrived in London? Why had she held herself aloof—

—watching from a distance while he'd pretended to court other women.

Not as deep as the first, his second shock. This one of understanding, it pushed back against his rising anger. Cold prickles danced across his hands. Ernst flexed his fingers, mind racing. She hadn't greeted him upon her arrival in London. Instead, she had spied on him. The gossip must have reached her at the docks or at the latest, upon her arrival at the duchess's court, someone telling her of his dalliances. Delicious and cutting, that must have been, the sort of gossip session where every word stabbed through the heart and yet more such words had been sought. She'd listened to the gossip, and watched from a distance, only to have her worst fears confirmed.

For so it must have seemed. He'd pretended to court Beryl Wentworth in March, Coralie Busche in October, and while both had ended with announcements of the given ladies' marriages, followed by the actual ceremonies and him vanishing from their lives, both must have seemed to herald the end of the world to the poor woman hiding from his presence. And only yesterday the *Chatterer* had carried news of his own engagement, albeit not with his agreement. It must have seemed as if he sought a woman, any woman, to replace the love he'd lost, as if he'd given up hope of ever finding her again.

The ache deepened, anger and shock fading. With his games he'd bruised her. By helping those young ladies find their loves and settle their lives, he'd destroyed his own. More importantly, he'd destroyed hers. He'd wondered what the acid of his games had eaten into. Not his code of ethics, not even his honor—it had been his love.

And the coldest irony of all—if he'd bothered to attend any function at the Duchess of Brittany's court-in-exile during the long summer just past, he'd have seen her. A maid of honor could not have absented herself from a formal event.

He had to explain.

Sane reason flooded him, finally. Ernst continued down the stairs, toward his impatient stallion and the curious, staring groom.

If he thundered into her presence, demanding her attention and spewing out excuses, he'd finish driving her away. Her proud, rebellious temper had never responded well to outside pressure, and he refused to make that mistake.

No, he'd woo her. All the experience he'd gained from playing his matchmaking game could be put to good use. She liked beautiful clothing, dances, being made much of with honest attention and fetching of ices and deep conversation. She liked knowing she was loved.

None of that would be any punishment to him, even if it forced him to attend formal functions among the French *émigrés*. They whispered secrets, both military and political, hoping to win favor from their ducal patroness and her royal cousin beyond—

and it didn't always matter if the secrets they whispered should be shared. It didn't even matter that the secrets be true, only the illusion they created, if that illusion could possibly please the Duchess of Brittany or the Duke of Orléans.

If any of Napoleon's spies remained in London, that was where they'd be, trying to blend in and not be caught. But that didn't matter any longer. Ursula attended the duchess at her court-in-exile. Despite the danger, to court he would go.

A deep breath settled his plan and his soul. The groom held the far stirrup and he mounted. Then Ernst kneed the big warhorse and Sassenach broke into a willing canter, heading back to London.

The End

Author's Note

All Biblical quotations are from the Tynedale New Testament of 1530, courtesy Project Gutenberg. In this, the first translation of the New Testament into English, the text of 1st Corinthians 13:4–8 reads:

Love suffereth long, and is courteous. Love envieth not. Love doth not frowardly, swelleth not, dealeth not dishonestly, seeketh not her own, is not provoked to anger, thinketh not evil, rejoiceth not in iniquity: but rejoiceth in the truth, suffereth all things, believeth all things, hopeth all things, endureth in all things. Though that prophesying fail, or tongues shall cease, or knowledge vanish away: yet love falleth never away.

About the Author

Vivian Roycroft is a pseudonym for historical fiction and adventure writer J. Gunnar Grey. And if she's not careful, her pseudonymous pseudonym will have its own pseudonym soon, too—along with a Kindle stuffed with Jane Austen and Patrick O'Brian stories, a yarn stash, and a turtle sundae at Culver's.

Also by Vivian Roycroft

for children
Sydney and Leyton's Great Adventure

Regency standalone
Love, Unmasked

Regency series: The Scoundrel of Mayfair
Scandal on Half Moon Street
Mischief on Albemarle
Shenanigans in Berkeley Square
Whispers on the Hampstead Road

Regency series: Love in Napoleon's War
A Different Sort of Perfect

Have you read...?

Lady Clara Huckabee trembled. She felt it in her traitorous knees, which threatened to deposit her in an undignified heap on the Grecian Axminster carpet, and in her throat, tightened almost unbearably beneath her morning gown's simple velvet neckline. Disappointing her guardian was bad enough, but since he started this fiasco, surely he'd endeavor to bear it. Shocking her aunt, though—for shocking Clara's response would be—was far worse, because it must necessarily cause a measure of pain and Aunt Helen's sweet soul outweighed her silly, old-fashioned notions. Clara steeled herself. It was their actions, their insistence, which forced her to this miserable necessity. If they refused to consider her wishes in the selection of a husband, *her* husband, then they must accept some of the blame for the contretemps that ensued.

Hopefully the housekeeper wasn't listening behind the closed drawing room door.

A deep breath, and Clara softened her clenched hands into gentler folds. Only then did she trust herself to meet the Viscount Maynard's black eyes, unblinking and glittering. No matter how many times she ordered herself to be meek and affable, he still looked like a possessive lizard.

"It distresses me to cause grief in anyone, particularly a gentleman as eminent as my Lord Maynard, and I find no pleasure in disappointing my esteemed aunt and uncle." She paused. Those reptilian eyes widened and bulged; perhaps she was the first person to dare cross the arrogant booby. Clara hurried on before she could be interrupted. "However, the selection of a lifetime partner is too delicate an operation to be entrusted to any third party, no matter how revered. Kingdoms will neither rise nor fall on my lineage and therefore I believe my own desires and tastes should be consulted. I am sorry, but I cannot accept my lord's offer of marriage."

Viscount Maynard's gaze drifted from her face, drifted lower. "The child has an opinion of her own." When he'd asked for her hand, his voice had been courteous and correct; now he drawled his words, taking twice as long to state a simple sentence. His lips curled as if he smelled something unspeakable. "How precocious."

Her skin crawled. His gaze boasted weight and mass, as if his hand explored her body without permission. So much for meek and affable; the viscount was surely more interested in her inheritance, in Papa's money, than in her or her hand. "My lord, your anxiety to change my opinion *must* be un-bounded." She dropped her most formal curtsey and escaped from the drawing room. Let him eat cake; just not hers.

After the drawing room's sun-drenched warmth, the cool Grecian elegance of the entryway made her face feel hot. If the housekeeper had bent her ear to the door, she'd run in time. With luck, Clara would escape, too, without additional arguments. But on the curved stairway's far side, the library door stood ajar. That would be Uncle David's temporary retreat and he'd be listening for the first sign of movement. Yes, there was his shadow, approaching the door-way. No time to spare.

Clara composed her expression as she ran up the white marble stairs, her slippers soundless, her pale muslin skirt gathered in one hand and her other trailing up the ebony banister. A few moments alone, hidden in the old schoolroom where Papa had taught her mathematics and the stars, and she'd compose herself. Their little telescope was still there, beneath the heavy canvas covering they'd sewn for it, pointing as he'd left it to the merchant shipping and men-of-war anchored in the Sound. If she held the canvas close to her face and breathed deeply, sometimes it seemed she could still smell his musky scent on the neat stitching, so much more even than her own. The memory cooled her temper, but did nothing for the hole he had left behind in her heart. She'd always miss him, always, and no man—certainly not that titled twaddle—could ever remove him from the foremost place in her heart.

Aunt Helen waited at the top of the stairs, almost dancing in place. The artless little brunette wisps fallen from her upturned hair framed her delighted smile, and she held out her hands as Clara paused, three steps below. Surely Aunt Helen, with her superb taste, hadn't presumed she'd accept that man?

"Our viscountess-to-be! My beautiful niece, I wish you joy."

It was inexplicable, but it seemed to be horribly true. "In regard to my fortunate escape, I'm sure." The tart words tumbled forth without thought. But there was no recalling them and while it had been dreadful imagining Aunt Helen's shock, seeing it only added a cold edge of satisfaction to Clara's anger.

"You didn't—you didn't refuse him? Clara, how could you?"

"With relief and a smile, I assure you. Dear aunt, how could you imagine I'd agree to marry anyone so cold and arrogant?"

"But he is a viscount. The ways of the nobility are not like ours. Great wealth and vast landholdings, dating from generations long gone, give a nobleman a sense of entitlement that you and I cannot understand. He would make an excellent husband for you."

The anger broke through her restraint like floodwaters rushing from a collapsing dam. "I am no entitlement. Aunt Helen, could you marry without love?"

"Oh, Clara." Aunt Helen tucked the fallen curls behind her ears. "Not that again. We've had this discussion over and over—"

"You will never convince me."

"—and while it's a wonderful, romantic notion to marry for love rather than for stability, fortune, or position, it's simply not practical. You must have a husband—"

"An encumbrance I know only too well."

"—and it will not be the Frenchman."

That was a new voice, a masculine, booming one, coming from the stairs behind her. Clara whirled. Uncle David had approached to within two steps, and she hadn't heard his footfall through her temper tantrum and their raised voices. His blue eyes, usually warm despite their cool deep color, now burned like chips of Arctic glacial ice.

"Uncle—"

"We are at war with France," Uncle David said, "a fact you seem able to forget but which torments my every hour, waking or sleeping. Your father's ships—your fading inheritance—are being taken, sunk, burned, destroyed, and your father's sailors are wasting away and dying in Napoleon's prison hulks." He stepped closer, and while he wasn't a tall man, in this tempestuous state he seemed twice as large as life, and she seemed smaller. "I will see you unmarried and disinherited before I allow you to wed a Frenchman."

His declaration rang through the stairwell and entry. Aunt Helen stepped back, hand to her throat. Clara gripped the banister. He would not make her cry. And she would not allow him to win.

"Viscount Maynard has been so good as to accept my invitation to supper and cards." Uncle David's voice, while quieter, surrendered none of its authoritative ice. "We agreed that not every immediate refusal equates to an absolute no."

Again her knees threatened to deposit her, this time onto the white marble. And this time was far worse. She would not cry, no matter what he said.

"You will go to your room and consider the viscount's proposal in greater depth." He turned and clattered down the stairs, the tails of his claret-colored coat fluttering with each step.

No tears. And he would not win.

Clara threw the inoffensive morning dress onto the floor and, in her shift, rang for fresh water.

"Take that rag away, Nan, please."

The maid picked up the muslin, nervous hands folding and refolding it. "Shall I have it cleaned, miss?"

"No. Throw it out. Give it to the poorhouse. Keep it for yourself. But get rid of it. I'll never wear it again."

Alone, she sponged the lingering stain of those hungering reptilian eyes from her skin, washing again and again until she finally felt clean. The cold way he'd leered at her, as if she were a broodmare at auction, mouth open to be checked! Clara shivered. Did that ugly, open sort of scrutiny best symbolize the marriage market? None of the gentlemen in her usual set, and certainly none of the Frenchmen she'd met during the too-short Amiens peace, had ever looked at her in such a lewd manner. It was not to be borne.

The *marriage market*. That was Diana Mallory's term for it, this desperate seeking for a powerful, rich, fashionable husband, and Diana had seen enough of it in London to not complain when her parents moved her to Plymouth. So long as they returned to London for the season, of course. And oh, the horrifying stories she'd told; poor Harmony Barlow's jaw had hung open like a fly trap. It had seemed so hilarious from that safe distance. Now, her giggles were quite gone.

Hands trembling still, Clara pulled on a clean shift—Nan could have the old one, as well as the dress—short stays that tied in front, and a petticoat. When she reached into the wardrobe, it wasn't to her other morning gowns, on the left, but to the walking gowns, in the center. She crushed her favorite grey sarsnet to her bodice. Uncle David had told her to go to her room and think. He hadn't told her to stay there. And she was finished thinking, at least as far as the viscount was concerned. Perhaps she'd better vanish for a while, until the household's broiling emotions cooled and soothed. Too bad she couldn't simply vanish and return, happily married to the perfect man, on the day before her nineteenth birthday, five months hence.

She tugged on the round dress, the colorless color of diffused shadows, trimmed with light dove crepe. She added the matching bonnet, a silk wrap, and pale kid gloves, grabbed her lace-making kit for luck, and snuck down the back stairs. The housekeeper and Nan bustled past in the hallway, gossiping in such low tones that all Clara could hear was her name; indeed the blasted woman had listened outside the drawing room door for quite long enough. Once the horizon was clear, Clara slipped out the back window, guilt and smug naughtiness fighting for dominance. She hurried across Ker Street in the face of an oncoming hackney coach and joined the pedestrian flow toward Plymouth Dock.

The fresh breeze tried to snatch her shawl away, billowing the silk behind her, and she tightened it about her arms. The bonnet's brim shaded her eyes from the noonday light, but welcome summer warmth reached her face when she tilted up her chin. Behind her, the assembly hall and shops tempted, a promising source of news and fun. Perhaps the latest fashion plates had arrived from Paris, and if so, Harmony and Diana would have something droll to say about them. But it was likely that the viscount had discussed his intended marriage with his friend Colonel Durbin, who would of course tell Mrs. Durbin, which meant Miss Dersingham and therefore everyone else in town knew about it, too. Better to avoid the popular places until she felt more capable of speaking rationally on the subject; Harmony and Diana would consider her scrape just as worthy of their wit. While there was a ridiculous side to the affair, she wasn't yet prepared to discuss it.

It was impossible to think on private woes while walking a public street. She hurried on, determinedly keeping her mind and features a composed, sociable blank. As she neared the Dock, the ocean's scent counterbalanced the horses and coal-smoke. The houses crowded together and the streets narrowed. But before respectability deteriorated too far, a mews opened to the side. Clara ducked inside, away from the lane. Halfway down the long, low building stood a faded yellow door, locked, of course. But Paul, Papa's one-time stable boy, had taught Harmony and her how to open it during their long-ago hoyden days. A shake of her wrist while turning, one hard push, and the door clacked open in defeat.

Inside was dark as the darkest night, quieter than the streets, and the slice of brilliant sunshine cutting through the open door revealed dust-cloth-covered lumps—long sofas and loungers, high-backed, old-fashioned wingchairs, stubby little tables for teas long gone. She and Paul used to peer beneath the white sheets at the fine old furniture, giggling and sneezing as dust flew about them, Harmony worrying her fingernails and hanging on her heel in the doorjamb, ready to run at the first hint of trouble and adamant no dust would touch her white gossamer gown. No one had ever come near, though.

They'd had so much fun together. But then Papa had died, all the horses but two had been sold, Paul had been let go, Harmony had convinced her to turn up her hair and attend to fashion, and high-society Diana had taken Paul's place in their little trio. When Uncle David had written Paul's reference, he'd printed *finis* to her childhood.

Without her consent, tears blurred the mounded shapes around her. She left the door on the latch for what little light it offered and slipped through the silent aisles, her wrap catching on a dressing table and raising dust that tickled her nose toward a sneeze. In the nearest corner, a large, cone-shaped bundle hung from the rafter, covered from hook to bottom with aged canvas and bound with cleverly knotted ropes. Clara slid beneath the canvas's folded and stitched edge, twisting to fit beneath the knots—it felt tighter than it used to be, or was she larger? She squeezed inside anyway. Beneath the covering, rippling softness slid across her cheek and clavicle, and she settled cross-legged within the hanging chair's satin draperies. Here, in her secret place, gently rocking, away from everyone, with no sights or stray sounds to distract her, finally she could think.

Why, *why* had Papa written that odious clause into his will? She wanted his money, of course she did—it was her inheritance by birthright. But she would only inherit if she married before her nineteenth birthday, less than half a year away, and that meant she had to marry with Uncle David's permission and approval. Her time was running out. And the only man she'd ever want to marry was so far out of her reach, he might as well be dead.

Sobs broke through and she crumpled her handkerchief to her face. Phillippe. Captain Phillippe Levasseur, beyond elegant in his pristine breeches, blue uniform coat trimmed with gold bullion and white lace. Those careless auburn locks, cut short in the modern Brutus manner, had cascaded over his smooth-cream forehead. His commanding dark eyes had never left hers as he bowed over her hand when Diana's older brother introduced them in the assembly room. She'd been weak-kneed then, oh, indeed. If he'd commanded her to wed him at that moment, she'd have taken his arm without hesitation.

Everyone in her set knew he was perfect, had said so time and again. He'd danced the first *six* with her at the Mallorys' ball, setting tongues wagging throughout the three towns, and Uncle David had scolded her for the imprudence. Phillippe had taken to calling on the Barlows every Tuesday, when he knew she'd be there, too, and they hadn't been able to claim their meetings at the assembly room were accidental for long. Of course his political views were odd, republican and democratic and so on, but surely his charm and delightful manners made up for all that. And the possibilities once she married into a chateau and vineyard in France!

But the peace had collapsed more than a year ago. She'd heard nothing, *nothing* from him since then. Fashion plates could cross from France, Royal Society fellows traveled back and forth as they pleased. But the tear-stained notes she wrote him could only be burned.

How could an odious viscount, or even a duke, compare with perfection? And how could Uncle David expect her to marry that brute? Uncle David had been so kind when he'd first arrived in Plymouth to care for her, sitting quietly in the music room while she'd poured out her heart through the harp and pianoforte. He'd told her stories of Papa's years at sea, during the American war and the early days of the revolution in France. But he'd grown quieter during the brief year of peace and as she'd neared her penultimate birthday, he'd set himself to select her husband, as if he couldn't wait to be shot of her. As if she couldn't be trusted to select her own husband perfectly well.

She wiped her eyes and fought the tears. Viscount Maynard was out of the question. But she did need a husband. She could pray for peace, final, blessed peace, and wait for Phillippe. But if peace took too much time, she'd lose Papa's home, the rooms where they'd played and watched ships in the harbor, everything he'd intended for her. Or she could marry someone less than perfect.

Hinges creaked, not nearby. A hollow boom echoed in the warehouse's cavern. Clara gasped. Even her tears froze as footsteps approached. No one had ever interrupted before, in all the years she'd visited the warehouse. It almost seemed a sign.

"Lousy trespassing brats must have left the door open again. Yes, right, that one there." The Cheapside voice made no pretension toward being anything but mercantile. "And these. They're to go to the *Topaze,* out in the Sound. Oh, and that hanging thing. Be careful with it, Clumsy Joe."

The chair swung, rocked, rocked again, jolted up and back. Clara grabbed the wooden frame, her heart pounding so loudly it seemed impossible they didn't hear it.

"Heavier than it looks, mate."

And then the hanging chair floated free, the unseen footsteps' owners carrying it—and her—away.

It would be humiliating, but she had to say something before she wound up on board a ship. She opened her mouth.

No sound emerged. Her voice refused. She closed her mouth, rolling her lips together.

A ship. A ship could take her anywhere, including France. Across the seven seas, in search of her perfect Phillippe.

She could vanish for more than a few hours, indeed for as long as it took. She could find him, marry him, bring him home to Uncle David, a *fait ac-*

compli.

But there was Aunt Helen to consider, and even Uncle David. They'd worry when she vanished, when they discovered she was gone. Her heart hardened. It would serve them right. How could they imagine they knew what was best for her when they refused to even consider her wishes?

It was a wild, a desperate gamble. But her situation was dire.

And she wouldn't have to see the miserable viscount again, for dinner, cards, or anything else.

Simply as that, she had a third option.

Thanks for reading! Dingbat Publishing strives to bring you quality entertainment that doesn't take itself too seriously. I mean honestly, with a name like that, our books have to be good or we're going to be laughed at. Or maybe both.

If you enjoyed this book, the best thing you can do is buy a million more copies and give them to all your friends... erm, leave a review on the readers' website of your preference. All authors love feedback and we take reviews from readers like you seriously. And if you believe that, then feel free to buy a million more copies and give them to all your once and future friends. Not to mention the past ones who will never speak to you again.

Oh, and c'mon over to our website:

www.DingbatPublishing.ninja

Who knows what other books you'll find there?

Cheers,

Gunnar Grey,
publisher, author, and Chief Dingbat

δ

www.ingramcontent.com/pod-product-compliance
Lightning Source LLC
Chambersburg PA
CBHW061257120726
48001CB00001B/347